Ignorant Souls

By

Richard Jeanty

RJ Publications, LLC

Newark, New Jersey

The characters and events in this book are fictitious. Any resemblance to actual persons, living or dead is purely coincidental.

RJ Publications
richjeanty@yahoo.com
www.rjpublications.com
Copyright © 2009 by Richard Jeanty
All Rights Reserved
ISBN 0-9817773-4-1
978-0981777344

Printed in Canada

Octoberber 2009

1 2 3 4 5 6 7 8 9 10

DEDICATION

This Book is dedicated to the memory of Lloyd E. Hart, Jr. of The Black Library

How easily we forget? I can never forget you, bro.
You were the reason I used to enjoy coming to Boston for booksignings.
Kicking it with you on Washington Street by your stand as the readers come by.
We didn't just talk about books, but about life in general.
I would go up the street to see you when my daughter was in the hospital.
Your encouraging words would make me feel like everything would be okay.
Well, everything is okay as you said. My daughter is now in school, doing well.
You created something that was special and many people miss it and you.
Booksignings in Boston have never been the same without you.
There's no need to go to Boston as often anymore.
I don't have anybody to kick it with while I wait for a reader to show up anymore
I don't get advice about life anymore the way you used to do it.
I don't meet too many people offering jobs to kids to keep them off the streets like you did.
Even though you weren't rich, you gave much of the little you had.

I'm sure that heaven was happy to have you, but you're surely missed on earth.

Rest in peace my brother.

ACKNOWLEDGEMENTS

I would like to thank all the usual suspects who have supported me through my writing career and other endeavors. You know who you are.

To my baby girl, Rishanna, I will always love you unconditionally. Thanks for coming into my life. Special "thanks" goes out to my dad for always showing a lot of enthusiasm about my work.

Special thanks go out to all the book clubs and readers who continue to inspire me to get better with each book. I would like to give a big shout- out to the street vendors and booksellers around the country and all over the world for keeping the world in tune with our literature. Thanks to all the book retailers and distributors who make it possible for our books to reach the people.

A special shout-out goes to all the New York book vendors and entrepreneurs. Special thanks to Chanel Caraway and Makisha Cheeks for taking the time to read the manuscript.

A big shout-out goes out to my nephews and nieces as well as my brothers and sisters.

A special shout out goes to the best assistant in the world, Yolander Boston.

This book is also dedicated to all the brothers on lockdown. Come home and change your life for the better. These black children need their fathers. You can still teach them right from wrong.

Introduction

The word "Ignorant" is defined as exhibiting lack of education and knowledge; being unaware and uninformed, according to Webster's dictionary.

To be honest, I'm not quite sure that this definition is completely accurate. Sometimes I feel completely unaware and uninformed about a lot of issues in my own life. I also feel uneducated and unknowledgeable about many subjects at times. Though formally educated, however, whenever I feel that way, I make it my personal business to educate myself, become aware, informed and knowledgeable of the things that I don't know.

As I get older, I'm finding that life has to be balanced and the only way for any of us to maintain that balance, we have to continue to educate ourselves. I'm not talking about formal education in a school setting necessarily, but to educate ourselves in a way that would broaden our awareness in the world.

Many of us are walking around ignorant for no reason, and most of the time we are blinded by our own ignorance. I wanted to write a book about the darkness that some people in society live in, without actually even knowing it. In America, we are told that democracy is the way to go and everyone should have a certain level of tolerance and understanding towards each other. If that's the case, that basically means that we are all supposed to be on par with each other as well, intellectually, educationally and may be even financially.

How can that work in a society where a certain group of people seem to be the ruling majority? How can some of us emerge from darkness without the proper resources and tools that would enable such progress?

The highschool that attended was so far behind educationally, I'm surprised I even made it through college, sometimes.

This introduction could be very long because I have a lot of questions, but I will just stop here because there will be far too many answers as every single one of us sees things very differently in life.

Chapter 1
Knowing Nothing Better

Buck's grandfather had nothing to do with his status as a slave. He had come from a generation of slaves captured off the coast of Africa by greedy western explorers who wanted to exploit them in the new world. His grandfather never knew his original African name, because he carried the name given to him by his master from the transcontinental trip across the Atlantic hundreds of years prior. The last name Johnson became the name that he was identified by, but his first name was Earl. When President Abraham Lincoln signed "The Emancipation Proclamation," Earl was faced with a very tough decision. Having worked for the Johnson family since he was old enough, or should I say young enough to utter his first word, he knew no other world. A small shack built on the plantation where he worked was referred to as the "slave quarters." Earl and his family worked the land for the very wealthy Mr. Johnson, but he was compensated with things only fit for an animal in society at the time.

The auction of his dad to a different family when he turned fourteen years old forever separated Earl from his blood kin. He became a man very early in his life. His father had taught him how to work the land and harvest corn for the Johnsons as well as cotton. By the age of sixteen, Earl had started his own family with a young woman named Mabel who was the child of a slave owned by the neighbors down the street. Earl was a big black boy, standing 6-ft-3 inches tall by the age of fourteen. The white family who owned him and his parents felt he was big and strong enough to carry on the duties of his father by himself. Thus, they sold his father to another family to make even more money. When Lincoln announced that the slaves were freed Earl was twenty-four years old, but there was no record to prove his actual age. He and Mabel had a five-year old son named Bill and another son named Gethro. With two mouths to feed, and no ownership of any land, Earl had to figure out a way to help support his family. It was a joyous day as the slaves gathered at their local church to chant, "We's free. We's free." The joy of freedom soon faded away as the slaves learned that the forty acres and a mule promised to them would not be delivered by the federal government.

What was Earl to do? Where was he going? How was he gonna eat or feed his family? Or worse, what was he going to do about the harassment from the Ku Klux Klan? All those things played a factor in Earl's decision to remain a slave voluntarily. Though his situation was far from luxurious, he had a job that provided him with food and shelter at the time. There were other brave slaves who chose to leave their masters and search for new life elsewhere, but Earl wasn't that brave. He wished he could've linked up with his mother and father so they could start a new life together as a family unit somewhere else, but his master wouldn't reveal to him who his mom and dad were sold to. By then, his mom and dad were long gone to Virginia and Earl had no way to get there. He didn't even know where Virginia was located on the map.

His master went from allowing him the scraps like pig intestines, corn meal, grits and pig feet to having chicken legs. The funny thing about pig intestines that Earl didn't know was that it was his master's way of degrading him and his family. Black people would eventually develop a love affair with pig intestines better known as "chitlins'" but most of them don't realize the story behind it. It wasn't until years later that Earl would explain to his son Bill that chitlins were something that the slave masters enjoyed watching the slaves eat. It could not get any more degrading than watching their black servants, whom they considered less than human, eat the worst part of the pig. The intestine is where the pig defecates and whites took joy in watching black people clean and cook that part of the pig to eat it. Most of the time, they would vomit at the smell of chitlins cooking and would laugh because black folks had to eat it. Grits were no different. Grits and corn meal were just as demeaning as chitlins, because white people would not eat them. They in turn gave it to their black slaves as satisfying foods. It took Earl a long time to figure all that out, but he eventually did. However, it didn't stop him from continuing to eat grits, corn meal and chitlins. Black folks made the best of the scraps that were given to them for survival sake.

Though Earl became a voluntary slave, he became wise enough as time went by and vowed that his kids would not stay in slavery. He decided to make a deal with Mr. Johnson and that deal landed him ten acres of land, which he eventually passed on to his boys, Bill and Gethro. Black people were the best farmers in the South at the time and Mr. Johnson couldn't find anybody to work his land for him as well as Earl did. He agreed to sell ten acres to Earl with a payment plan over fifty years. In return, Earl had to work the other hundred plus acres of farm land that Mr. Johnson owned. Earl trusted that the document Mr. Johnson had his attorney draw up was legit and he signed it with an X as he was illiterate and could not translate the document to understand it. Mr. Johnson basically secured another fifty years of free labor and Earl thought that his boys would be land owners after he passed on. Mr. Johnson and his lawyers plotted and the document only stated that Earl and his family could stay on his property for fifty years as long as they continued to harvest his land, and if for any reason they refused to continue to work his land, he had the right to kick them off.

There was contempt on Earl's part even though he wanted to believe Mr. Johnson, somewhat. Years earlier, Earl had watched his father take a beating at the hand of Mr. Johnson because his daughter had reported to him that his father looked at her in a funny, sexual way. The leather lasso against his father's back drew blood instantaneously. Mr. Johnson was trying to teach him a lesson and he made sure that his children stood around to watch because they would be served the same fate if they ever crossed the line with Mr. Johnson's children and grandchildren.

The reality of the situation was that Mr. Johnson's daughter
was a little "Too Hot to Trot" Jezebel who had heard that
the slaves walked around with penises as large as a horse's.
She had been sleeping around with a white boy who did
nothing for her, and one day while Earl's dad took a break
from working under the hot sun to take a leak against a tree,
which he thought shielded, his penis from view, Mr.
Johnson's daughter was gawking at it and couldn't stop
talking about it since. She kept harassing him to see it up
close, but he wouldn't let her. Every day she would walk
almost a mile to where Earl's father was working to ask him
if he could pull it out and let her see, but he refused every
time. She eventually got tired of asking and that's when she
went to her dad and made up the story about him looking at
her in a sexual way.

That incident stained Earl's mind forever and he was
reluctant to trust the Johnson family ever since. Earl would
eventually pass on at the age of fifty feeling that he had left
his family better off than he was. His two boys, Gethro and
Bill divided the ten acres of land between them. They would
work their parcel of the land after working Mr. Johnson's
everyday. The only thing they knew was the month and
year that land was to become theirs, and when that time
arrived, their father was long gone. It was then that they

discovered they never owned the land and they had to continue to work for Mr. Johnson for free in order to keep living on Mr. Johnson's property. Earl was still disciplined like a slave and his sons received the same form of punishment whenever Earl disapproved with something they did. Corporal punishment was the only way Earl knew how to discipline his boys and that cycle would linger on for generations to come. The sins of the old master continued to affect the lives of Earl's family.

While Bill decided to stay and work for the lying Mr. Johnson for a few more years, Gethro decided he had enough. He packed up his family and took them to Virginia, leaving Mississippi forever. There was more opportunity in Virginia for the newly freed slaves and Gethro knew that with his skills he could find a way to provide for his family. Bill would eventually leave a few years later to settle in Charleston, South Carolina. The two brothers never saw each other again.

Chapter 2
The Johnson Family

Buck Johnson grew up in Charleston, South Carolina in a small two-bedroom house on a farm that he shared with fourteen siblings. He dropped out of school in the sixth grade to help ease the financial burden on his mother. Buck Johnson was the fifth oldest of fifteen children and one of the most responsible kids of Bill Sr. and Fatima Johnson. At thirteen years old, Buck became the man of the house. His two older brothers didn't really care about the way their father treated them and their mother when the elder Johnson was alive. They left before Mr. Johnson beat the life out of them. His twin sisters ran away from the abuse when they were both sixteen years old. They married two brothers who moved them to Virginia to start a family. The elder Johnson was shot and killed, leaving his wife to raise eight younger children on her own. He was an habitual drinker who didn't know his limit. Bill Johnson Sr. was the meanest individual when he was sober and twice as mean when he was under the influence of alcohol.

Bill Johnson Jr., the eldest child of the Johnson couple, left home at the age of eighteen because he was tired of his father's abuse of his mother and the rest of the family. He didn't want to turn his back on his mother, but every time he urged her to leave, she would not leave his father. Bill Sr. worked hard during the day to provide for his family, but at night, it was a whole different story. A bottle of moonshine was his best friend and his wife was his doormat. Bill Sr. would force his wife to have sex against her will when he was drunk and he would get violent if she refused. The blows to Fatima's face were normalcy in that household. Every little argument ended up in a physical beating of his wife. He would get upset at her for getting pregnant so many times, but he had no idea how to pull out nor did he care.

Bill Sr. had beaten his wife so badly one night that Bill Jr., or BJ, as he was called by the family, had to intervene to save his mother. Bill Sr. knocked her unconscious because she told him she was too tired to have sex with him while she was pregnant. He told her, "No woman ain't never gonna say no to me when I wanna have me some. I be the one who pays for this house here and I be the man of the house." Mrs. Fatima Johnson could only cry and wished that her baby wasn't dead from all the pounding she suffered at her husband's hand. When BJ saw his father hurting his mother, he pushed him to the ground to get her away from him. While still in his drunken state, Bill Sr. told his son, BJ, to get out of his house and if he didn't leave he was gonna get his rifle and shoot him.

BJ cried as he packed his suitcase with the two dress shirts and pants that his mother had sewn for him. He begged his mother to leave with him, but she told him that she couldn't turn her back on her babies. Her other children were still young and very dependent on their mother, as she was the only nurturing person in their lives. Bill Sr. wouldn't have been able to care for those kids, anyway, because the only thing he knew other than drinking was farming, which he forced all his kids to do everyday when they got home from school. When BJ left, his mother gave him all the money that she had saved, which was ten dollars. He had his mind set on New York City, but ten dollars was very limited even in the 1940's.

BJ was the biggest dreamer of all the Johnson kids. He wanted to become a playwright since he was a child. He abhorred his father because his dad pulled him out of school after he completed eighth grade. BJ believed that his father had cut his dreams short because his father never went to school to learn to read. His father didn't like the fact that he couldn't read his own mail even though he called himself the man of the house. He used to also get upset when BJ would try and teach his mother how to read better. Bill Sr. didn't want anyone in his family to know more than he knew. He resented the fact that he had to work the field all his life. Fatima was happy to send her kids to school so they could have a better life than she did.

Bill Sr.'s resentment was just, at times. Having grown up in the field and saw nothing but maltreatment at the hands of his father, Earl, who was a former slave bamboozled by his former owner who tricked him into working for free for many years so he could attain his independence and a better life for his family. His father was beaten and disciplined for being lazy even when he spent twelve to fourteen hours on the field picking cotton, while the slave master sat on the porch drinking lemonade in the shade. Earl Johnson was proud and had integrity. He knew how hard he worked for that white man. He raised his son, Bill, to be a hard and proven worker so that no white man could ever call him lazy. When Earl had to discipline Bill, he knew no other way to deal with him, except for the old ways of the master. The whip that marked his back for many years became the whip that marked his children's backs. The forbiddance of an education was also a repeated cycle in Bill Sr.'s life, because his father would beat him and tell him that he had no right to be smarter than him. Bill Sr. just couldn't break the cycle with his own children.

After BJ left the house, his father continued to abuse his mother and the second oldest of their children, Gerald, who was about seventeen years old. Unlike BJ, Gerald was not afraid of his father. Every time his father would hit him he would stand there and take his punches like they meant nothing. However, whenever his dad would beat on his mother, he would go and run behind the house. He couldn't stand there and watch his father beat on his mom. One night Bill Sr. was so drunk, he started beating on his wife with a belt because he didn't like the food that she had cooked. Gerald and Buck forcefully tackled their father and pulled the belt away from him. Bill Sr. didn't even have enough strength to get up from the floor. He lay passed out on the floor through the night.

The next day when Bill Sr. woke out of his drunken state, he gave Buck and Gerald the beating of their lives. He beat them so badly that they couldn't go to school for days. While Buck was hysterically crying through the whole beating, Gerald stood there and stared at his father without shedding a tear. Bill Sr. thought his belt was the answer to everything. Some of his kids managed to escape being beaten by him everyday, but Buck and Gerald were under their father's radar. Bill Sr. would beat Buck if he didn't bring him a glass of water fast enough while he was in the field. Gerald had gotten used to the beatings and lost respect for his father very early in his life. Bill Sr. was only able to instill fear in Buck with his belt. Buck didn't like the violent feeling of that belt against his premature skin.

The twin girls, Annie Mae and Aretha had their share of beatings as well, but when two young men who were visiting from Virginia offered them a better life in exchange for their hands in marriage, their mother urged them to get married to get away from their father. At sixteen years old, they didn't need their parents' approval to go up to Virginia to get married. They ended up sharing a two-bedroom house with the two brothers who were also farmers. The two men were in their late twenties and they came down to South Carolina to visit some family members when they ran into the girls in town. They owned a small parcel of land that was left by their dad. They grew cotton and raised cows. It wasn't a luxurious life, but the men would go on to take great care of the two sisters. The two brothers eventually built another house on the land so they could each have their own homes.

Gerald loathed his father so much, not because of the beatings he suffered at his father's hand, but because of the maltreatment of his mother by him. Bill Sr. had driven his first and oldest son out of the house and Gerald appeared to have been following the same path as his brother. It was a matter of time before Gerald exploded, as his father was making the situation at home worse for him. The drunker Bill Sr. became the more he beat on his wife and all his children were growing tired of it.

Mrs. Fatima Johnson was a courageous woman to stay with that man for as long as she did. Fatima wanted to show her children strength and dedication and in the process she put up with her husband's abusive behavior. Even though she woke up every morning and put her best face on, it was easy to tell that Fatima was suffering and the pain was starting to take a toll on her. It was bad enough that she had gotten pregnant every other year for the last twenty years while she had been with her husband, but his added abuse was wearing her thin.

Fatima found out she was pregnant with another child a couple of days after he had beaten her to a pulp. When she revealed to him that she was pregnant again he told her that she was a good for nothing harlot who could only have babies, during one of his drunk episodes. Bill Sr.

was also angry with Fatima and accused her of getting pregnant even though they could hardly feed the children they already had, as if he had nothing to do with it. He smacked her across the face and she ended up hitting her head on the cabinet above the kitchen sink. She was left with a big gash on her forehead and bleeding profusely while her two young sons, Gerald and Buck watched. It was the last time that Bill Sr. would ever raise his hands to Fatima.

Gerald was filled with anger and hate as he stood there watching his father denigrate his mother. Something came over him as he went to the back room, grabbed his father's .45-caliber shotgun, and blasted him across the chest, sending his father's body flying up against the kitchen wall. With tears running down his face, Gerald cocked the gun back and continued to release a barrage of bullets into his father until the gun was empty. By the time Buck and his other siblings grabbed the gun from Gerald, his father was laying dead against the wall, still with an angry, mean look on his face.

Gerald had had enough of his father taking his stress out on the family. All he could say to his mother was that he was tired of him beating on her and the rest of the family. Gerald reacted harshly because of his harsh environment.

Mrs. Johnson was mad that her husband had brought one of her kids to the brink of destruction, but she also knew that Gerald was not to blame. With blood still pouring down her face from her open gash, she grabbed her son and held him tightly in her arms to console him.

Chapter 3
American Justice

When the neighbors heard the gunshot blasts, they alerted the sheriff. When the sheriff arrived, they took Gerald into custody for the murder of his dad. Because there was no documented report of the abuse by his mother, Gerald was charged with first degree murder and manslaughter by the District Attorney. At his trial, his mother testified that his father had been abusive during her entire marriage and the whole family suffered as a result. However, the white court appointed attorney who represented Gerald was trying to force him to cop a plea instead of doing his job to demonstrate to the all-white jury that Gerald killed his father while defending his mother. His attorney did very little to convince the jury that Gerald was not a calculated murderer.

The jury deliberated for no more than fifteen minutes before they reached a verdict. After hearing from all the witnesses who were all children of the victim about the abuse they suffered at the hand of their father, the jury found Gerald guilty of manslaughter. The only reason they didn't find him guilty of murder was because the gash that Fatima received from hitting her head against the kitchen cabinet left a big scar on her forehead. The jury felt Mrs. Johnson should have taken the appropriate actions by reporting the beatings to the authorities. They also felt that Gerald took the law into his own hands and he had to face the consequences of his action. Gerald basically was sent to prison because a group of white people feared that if a black man could kill his father, there was no telling what he could do to them if they ever crossed the line with him in that community. Gerald was sentenced to twenty years in prison for defending his family against a cruel abuser. Two lives were destroyed in the Johnson household.

As tough as those white people down South wanted Fatima to believe they were, she felt they were the most cowardice people on the planet. They would harass unarmed black men for no reason, screaming racial epithets and all kinds of demeaning crap at them, but if those black men reacted to their harassment, they'd have to run back home and gather their baseball bats, guns and a mob to deal with them. "How can anybody call themselves tough when they have to rely on a mob of people and guns to defend themselves against unarmed people?" she often thought. A group of white people who wanted to take over his land once victimized her husband, but he stood his ground and fought. He was tied to the back of a truck once and left for dead, but he managed to survive and he became an even more violent man as a result. Her boys were constantly harassed and forced to run for their lives almost daily.

Fatima knew that Gerald was going to get lynched in court just like the other young men who got lynched walking home from school or church. She lived in a hostile environment down South and her husband learned the hostility from those same people who convicted his son for murder. Bill Sr. grew up watching his father and mother get whipped by their masters for no reason at all, most of the time. The white slave masters used physical abuse to keep their slaves submissive and as a result, Bill Sr. used the same tactics to discipline his family. He was a victim of circumstance and his son had also suffered from the same circumstances. The Johnsons are still suffering today from the remnants of slavery. While most white people refuse to believe that slavery has anything to do with the way black people live their lives today, the evidence is clear that the violent cycle they started many years ago with the forefathers continues to affect black people in the most devastating way. Fatima Johnson could testify to that.

White people created stigmas that are attached to the Johnson family today. Fatima Johnson ended up with so many children because her grandparents were forced to have many children to be born into slavery. Birth control was foreign to her illiterate family. Even today, some of her family members can't let go of the term "motherfucker" because they've gotten so used to being called that. One of her young daughters had the filthiest mouth. She picked up the cuss words while sitting on the steps of her white neighbor's house as a child, and they referred to black people as "motherfuckers," most of the time. Mrs. Johnson's mother told her how White people created that term when they used to force strong, young black men to sleep with their mother to create more black babies for their slave masters for the field, hence, the term "motherfucker". Her mother even explained the word "nigger" to her, but it was imbedded in their minds for so long, they had a hard time letting go of the word. Buck Johnson would later explain to his own grandchildren. "Sure, it's easy to say let's do away with that whole slave period, but I wonder how strong white people would be today if they suffered such cruel maltreatment for so many years. The Jews have a hard time dealing with about fifty years of cruelty and losing only a million people at the hand of Hitler, according to their own records. The Jews even have a museum now to remind them of the Holocaust. We can't even begin to compare the number of African lives that were lost during slavery, not to mention the amount murdered cold heartedly. What do Africans have to remind them of our Holocaust? Why are people so quick to tell them to forget about slavery? It's part of our history," he would say. It took Buck Johnson many years to finally obtain his wisdom, and he shared it with his grandchildren every chance he got.

Chapter 4
Man of the House

After Gerald was hauled off to jail for shooting his dad, Buck Johnson, the eldest of the children who stayed behind with his mother, became the man of the house. Buck Johnson was forced to leave school in order to help his mother raise his five brothers and three sisters. When Buck came to his mother with words that he wanted to leave school to help the family, his mother scolded him, but she also knew the reality of the situation was that she needed his help. As much as she thought she could work as a maid to clean rich White folks' houses, she was also pregnant with her last child and it was a matter of time before she would have to stop working so she could give birth.

The family hadn't heard from BJ since he left to pursue his dream as a playwright in New York. He didn't want to worry his mother too much about his struggles in New York City. BJ figured that the family would get along fine without him. He never even received the news that his father had passed. Buck wasn't worried about BJ coming back home to help the family. He wanted to make sure that his brothers and sisters, as well as his mother, were provided for. He was a very big kid for his age and he had mastered the art of farming from his father. It was the only good thing that came out of their relationship. His father worked closely with him to teach him everything he needed to know about farming.

Buck worked very hard to help his mother with household chores, bills and to help send his youngest siblings to school. Buck had also picked up a bad habit from his father. Even though he hated to receive beatings from his dad, Buck also used his belt to help discipline his younger siblings. Though his beatings weren't as harsh as the ones he suffered at the hand of his father, however, he used the same inhumane tactics.

By the time Buck reached the age of sixteen, he had two of his younger brothers, Daniel and Joseph who were also twins, ages fourteen helping him in the field when they got home from school. The family was doing okay financially, but not as well as when their father was alive. They never led a privileged life to begin with. The hand-me-down clothes had been a tradition in the Johnson family since the slavery days, but now it was worse because there weren't many clothes to hand down. By the time the younger kids got their hands on some clothes from the older kids, the material was usually falling apart, there were holes in them, and were destroyed altogether. Mrs. Johnson didn't have too much time on her hands to sew for her children after her husband died. Holding down a full-time job as a housekeeper and having to take care of nine children did not leave her much time to do anything else. Buck may have been the man of the house, but he also needed his mother's tender loving care at times as well. She always made him his favorite meals and lemonade after a long day's work in the field.

While Buck and his brothers did a tremendous job to help their mother financially, they weren't as efficient as their father. Also, the fact that they had a couple of bad weather seasons didn't help much with their crops. Because there was so little money available after Bill Sr. died, some of the children had to walk around barefoot and with the same clothes almost every day. Sometimes, they would take turns staying in the house naked in their underwear while the rest would wear the clothes that they had available outside on the field. Mrs. Fatima Johnson had to pay for her husband's funeral, the payment on the leased land, the mortgage for the house, and provide food and clothes for her children. It was a hard life for them for a while.

Chapter 5
The Prodigal Son Returns

It had been almost ten years since BJ left home with a small suitcase and ten dollars in his pocket. He hadn't spoken to his mother for at least five of those ten years. No one in the family knew what was going on with BJ. His mother prayed everyday that her son was okay and was hopeful that one day she would reunite with him. When BJ pulled up in front of his mother's house in a Cadillac, they wondered who he was. BJ had left home a little scrawny kid who weighed no more than one hundred and thirty pounds and stood at five feet and nine inches tall. He returned home a twenty-eight year-old man standing at six feet two inches tall and weighed one hundred and eighty pounds. There was a significant difference in the way BJ looked when he returned home. He looked like he had just stepped out of an upscale male magazine. He wore a white suit that was very sharp with a white shirt and brown tie to match his brown vest and brown and white shoes and brown hat. He was dressed like a scene out of one of those gangster movies from the twenties, which was considered sharp then.

No one recognized the man wearing the expensive white suit and driving the expensive car. They all thought it was someone coming to kick them out of their house because Mrs. Johnson was a couple of months behind on her mortgage payments. When BJ walked up the stairs that Sunday afternoon and stood in the kitchen to watch his mother still slaving over the stove cooking some of his favorite food for the rest of the children, he could not believe his eyes. She had deteriorated to almost nothing. She looked tired, underweight and worn out. Life had taken its toll on his mother for the last ten years. A part of BJ was sad to see his mother like that, but he was also overtaken by the joy of seeing her again. Tears flooded his face. He had mixed emotions. The tears were a combination of sadness and joy.

He just stood there watching his mom and the three grown girls he assumed were his younger sisters. They also stood around looking mesmerized by the rich man in the nice outfit. Buck and the twin boys were out in the field working. BJ's youngest siblings didn't really know much about him because he had left home when one of them was very young and the other was still in the womb. The two children in the kitchen who were both girls ranged from age seven to nine. They had no idea that the man they were staring at was their older brother. Mrs. Johnson finally turned around to see why all was quiet in her kitchen. Like any mother who had not seen her son in a long time, Mrs. Johnson was hysterically happy to see her first-born came back to South Carolina to see her. It could've been hundreds of years later, she would still recognize her first child. She hugged him so tightly, it felt like she didn't want to let go as the tears flowed down her cheeks.

She had missed her eldest child. She wanted to touch his face, his hair and the new mustache that he was sporting. Her baby boy had grown up to be a handsome man and she missed most of it. She had longed to see Bill Jr. and she quickly introduced the girls to their brother. BJ was happy to meet both girls, one of which was born after he left. Mary, the nine-year-old asked, "Are you a doctor, mister?" Back then, it was customary for doctors in the South to dress very sharp everyday so people could acknowledge their social status. Mrs. Johnson sent Diana, the seven-year-old, to the field to get Buck and his brothers. BJ was elated to see his family again and when Buck finally arrived at the house, the two brothers ran towards each other for a long awaited hug. The younger twin brothers weren't sure what was going on, but BJ quickly reached his hand out to tell them that he was their older brother. They didn't recognize

BJ at first, but after a close look, they realized it was their brother. The other three girls were just flushed over the handsome man that they found out was their brother. "Are you rich?" asked Tabitha, the oldest of the three girls.

The whole family was overjoyed by the presence of BJ and his sophisticated appearance. But BJ quickly noticed that the twin girls and his brother Gerald were missing. The four of them were very close because they were closer in age from the rest of the children. It was with Gerald and the twins that BJ used to play "hide and seek" and every other game that they enjoyed. Mrs. Johnson didn't want to hit BJ with the bad news about his brother, but she had no choice. BJ also noticed that his dad was missing. He figured that his dad was working so hard in the field that he didn't want to walk away from his work to come see him. When BJ asked about his dad, the whole family was quiet. Mrs. Johnson let out a sigh of sadness before she told BJ that his father was dead.

BJ could not believe that he had missed his dad's funeral. Sure, he did not like the old man much for what he was doing to his family, but he wanted to be able to at least, pay his respect to the man. The worst news was yet to come. Mrs. Johnson did not want to go from one tragedy to the next, so she opted to tell BJ about his twin sisters who got married and moved to Virginia with their husbands. The girls wrote home regularly and Mrs. Johnson knew that they were doing well because the two brothers that they married bought an additional ten acres of land that they harvested themselves to produce some of the best cotton in Virginia. BJ was happy to hear that his sisters were doing so well. Mrs. Johnson also told him that he was an uncle because the twins had given birth to two boys each.

The moment of truth had arrived and BJ couldn't wait to hear how his brother was doing. When he asked his mother, "How's Gerald?" tears welled up in her eyes, as she told him that Gerald was in jail serving time for killing his father. BJ didn't have to ask his mother why Gerald had killed his father, because he had come close to killing the old man himself. He told his mother that she didn't have to explain anything to him because he knew that his father was abusive and it was a matter of time before one of the kids would kill him. With all the bad news that BJ was hearing, he wanted to change the subject to something lighter. BJ told his mother he didn't just come back to see her, but he came back to move the family up North to his new house in Rochester, New York.

BJ had finally caught a break and became an apprentice for a famous playwright in New York. He learned everything he could from the man who had taken him under his wing like a son. The man was very successful and had no family. When he fell ill, BJ took care of him and made sure that he received the best treatment at the hospital. Unfortunately, the man succumbed to his illness and left everything he owned to BJ, including the rights to his successful plays on Broadway. The man was very wealthy and successful and had written over ten plays that ran on Broadway for twenty years before his death. He had no next of kin and in his will, he left every single thing he owned to BJ, including his loft apartment in Greenwich Village where BJ spent most of his time.

Just like that, BJ had changed the mood in the house. Everybody was happy and BJ couldn't wait to get them to New York. He told his mother that she and the rest of the children could live in the ten-bedroom house in Rochester, New York because he spent most of his time at the apartment in Greenwich Village. He also told her that his brothers and sisters would all have jobs waiting for them with his new production company. BJ also wanted to know where his brother Gerald was being held so he could hire a better attorney to get a new trial for him.

BJ had to leave South Carolina a few days after he arrived because he needed to tend to his business back in New York. Before the old man died, he made BJ promise that he wouldn't sell the company under any circumstances. One of the most famous black playwrights to ever live, the man wanted to leave behind a legacy. He had taught BJ the day-to-day operation of the company and every detail that he needed to know over the last ten years in order for him to continue to strive, and BJ wanted to keep his promise to the old man. Before BJ departed for New York, he left a couple thousand dollars with his mother and gave her an address so she could have the family transported to New York in a couple of weeks.

Things were finally on the up side for the Johnson family and their future was looking brighter than ever. One of the first things BJ wanted for his family, was an education after they arrived in New York. The old man had taught him that education was the best way to earn respect in society. He had gotten his GED under the old man's tutelage and had also earned a Bachelor's Degree in theatre at night at City College.

A few months after the family moved to Rochester, the twin boys and the girls were all enrolled in the Rochester Public School system at night to earn their GED. However,

BJ hit a road block with Buck. Buck felt he was too old to return to school and to get ridiculed for things he couldn't do. His brother urged him to enroll in an adult program, but he continued to defy any suggestions made by his brother. Buck felt that school was not for him. He had grown accustomed to hiding his illiteracy and was eager to live his life as a man. The two younger girls attended school daily.

BJ had given Buck a job as an apprentice to the stage designer. Buck didn't like the job, but he stayed with it so he could earn enough money to find his own way in life. Theatre was never part of Buck's plan and stage designing wasn't something he even respected. He didn't understand why people would build something for a few weeks then tear it down for no reason. He had a short temper and he couldn't get along with the stage designer. One weekend while Buck took a ride with his brother to visit Boston, he took a liking to the city for some odd reason. BJ had brought his production to the Strand Theatre in Boston for a couple of weeks and brought Buck with him. Buck met a girl after the show that night.

Chapter 6
Buck Johnson

Buck was all smiles when they were leaving Boston, as he had made plans to go back to visit his new friend. Three months after visiting his new girlfriend, Esther, in Boston, Buck decided that he wanted to live in Boston to be near her. He had left her with enough money to secure a room for him before departing from his last visit. When Buck told his mother that he had met someone that he loved and wanted to be with her, she encouraged him to follow his heart. However, she didn't know that his heart was going to lead him to Boston. Although Mrs. Johnson was sad that she was going to lose yet another son to a new city, she also knew that Buck was a grown man who needed to make his own decisions and find his own way in life.

Buck told his brother, BJ, how grateful he was for all that he had done for him, but it was time for him to move on. As an older brother, BJ understood that his brother needed to make his own way in the world. He offered his brother a couple thousand dollars as a parting gift and told him to be careful in Boston because it was a racist city. The twin boys took Buck's departure especially hard because he had been their guide in everything that they did since their father died. They wished him well on his new journey. The girls loved their brother, but they didn't mind the fact that he was leaving because they would have one more place to visit during their summer vacation.

BJ had convinced Buck to learn to drive while he was in New York because he needed a chauffeur. Buck had turned down his job offer and his advice to get a license. With almost twenty five hundred dollars in his pocket, Buck took a bus to Boston along with his suitcase in hand and headed for his new life there. It was fall of 1966 when Buck left New York to join his new girlfriend in Boston. On the bus ride, all he kept thinking about was Esther and how he wanted to make her happy. Buck wanted to provide everything for Esther like his father did for his family, less the abuse. He wanted to get married, have children and buy a house for his new wife. But first, Buck needed to find a job when he got to Boston. He was contemplating working for a man who owed a favor to his brother, BJ, but that thought quickly faded because he wanted to do everything on his own. Independence had become very important to him.

When Buck arrived at the Greyhound bus station in downtown Boston, Esther was there waiting to welcome him to the new city. Buck suggested that they catch a cab to their destination, but Esther insisted that they take the bus so he could see the city. Still, Buck wanted to catch a cab because he was too tired to ride another bus. He wanted to get home as fast as possible. However, after standing there for almost fifteen minutes trying to hail a cab and being overlooked by about twenty different cabs that zoomed right pass him, he got the point she was making. He was really gullible to think that he was gonna be able to hail a cab as a black man in Boston in the sixties.

After another long bus ride around Boston, Buck finally reached his destination on Warren Street in Roxbury, Massachusetts. The place seemed a little strange at first because he had never seen so many huge Victorian homes on one street before. He settled in a rooming house that Esther was able to secure for about ten dollars a week. Esther helped fix the place to make it more homely for Buck, but she could never stay with him overnight. Esther came from a strict Christian home where her father didn't allow her to spend too much time with boys, even though she was eighteen years old.

Since Buck's residence had been taken care of, he wanted to make sure he found work so he could get his own home with the money that he brought with him. Buck was always good with his hands and was a fast learner. He searched around Boston for weeks looking for work and he couldn't catch a break. A few of the Black folks in Boston thought his southern accent was funny and country. It wasn't until he met another black man from South Carolina who owned a butcher shop on Blue Hill Avenue that Buck caught a break. The shop owner recognized the accent almost immediately and when he saw Buck walk into his shop, he knew that he had to say something to lift the young man's spirit because he looked like he was in a slump. The man was also from Charleston and found out through their conversation that he knew Buck's father.

The shop owner extended his hand to Buck and introduced himself as Mr. John Owens. Buck nervously shook the man's hand as he told him his name was Buck Johnson followed with a "sir". Mr. Owens told him that he didn't have to keep calling him sir and asked if there was anything he could do to help him. Buck told John that he had been looking for work for almost a month and things weren't looking very promising for him. Mr. Owens asked Buck if he had ever killed and stripped an animal before.

Buck told him that he grew up on a farm and he used to skin all types of animals. Mr. Owens offered Buck a job as a butcher and told him he could start the following Monday. He also explained to Buck that it was a lot of hard work with long hours and the pay wasn't going to be great. Buck didn't care one way or another because he only wanted a job.

After Buck landed a job, he went to a payphone and called Esther to tell her about his good fortune. He wanted to do something nice with her to celebrate. Esther suggested that they go to this soul food restaurant in Roxbury and a movie afterwards. Buck went to Esther's house to pick her up. Of course, he had to briefly meet her mother and he received the whole intimidating bit from her mom before leaving for their date. Her dad was not home at the time. They took the bus down to the restaurant. After eating, they both decided to go back to his rooming house to get to know each other better. Esther was still a virgin and Buck respected the fact that she wanted to do nothing more than necking with him. He had never kissed a woman before, but Esther brought out the voracity in him. He appeared a little anxious and rough, but Esther calmed him down and told him that she wasn't going anywhere and she was his to have, so he could take his time. After necking in the room for about two hours, which would've been the length of time for a movie, Buck decided to take Esther home.

He walked her up to the door at exactly nine o'clock in the evening, which was her weekend curfew. Her father opened the door to find a polite Buck standing there in a shirt and tie and a jacket with his hat in his hand. "My name is Earl Jamison," Esther's dad said. "Come on in, I wanna talk to you." "Yes sir," Buck answered. After Buck walked in the house, he was led to the living room. "Esther, can you get this young man something to drink," Earl said. "I don't need nothing, sir," Buck told him. "Okay then, young man. What I wanna know is, what's your intention with my daughter?" Earl said. "I don't got no intention, sir," Buck answered. "You better have some intentions because my daughter is not no loose woman you think you can just sleep with," Earl told him with certainty in his voice. "I ain't got no plan to sleep with her 'til we married, sir," Buck assured him. "So you do plan on marrying my daughter. That's good because that's the only way you gonna continue to see her. I ain't trying to raise no loose woman," Earl said.

Esther and her mother were in the kitchen while Buck and her dad were talking in the living room. "I really like him, mom. I hope daddy lets me go out with him again," Esther told her mother. "From the smile on your face, he must be a real nice young man. You know how your daddy get sometimes, but he's a good man and I'm sure he'll allow you to see this young man if he's as nice as you say he is," her mother assured her. "Mother, you know how daddy can be intimidating sometimes," she said. "I'll talk to him," her mother said with confidence.

Earl and Buck had great conversation about Esther and he felt comfortable enough with the southern boy to allow him to date his daughter. Buck was elated that he made such an impression on Mr. Jamison. It wasn't so much that he made an impression, he was well-mannered and respectful. Earl appreciated his southern characteristics and charm. Buck also discussed his plans to work hard so he could start his new life in Boston with Esther as soon as possible. Earl admired his courage to come all the way to Boston to start his own life, not only that, he also felt that Buck had to be very serious about his daughter to even decide to move to Boston for her.   During their conversation, Buck explained to Earl how he was infatuated with his daughter, from the moment he laid eyes on her. The only thing Earl stressed was the fact that they were a church-going family and in order for Buck to be part of that family, he had to start going to church on Sundays.

Buck left Esther's house that evening feeling envious of her family's camaraderie. Esther's parents were friendly with each other, something he wasn't used to seeing. He wanted to establish the same relationship with their daughter. Suddenly, Buck was excited about seeing Esther again, and perhaps being a permanent part of her life. He'd always planned to make her a permanent part of his life, but it was up to her to make him part of hers.

Chapter 7
Esther's Family

Earl and his family were also from the South. He moved his family from Macon, Georgia to Boston for a better life. While Earl may have been a devout Christian, he was also a man who ruled his house with an iron fist. He never had to physically discipline his children because his presence alone was intimidating. Standing at six feet five inches tall and two hundred and sixty pounds, the children knew not to cross him. However, he was also an open-minded man who understood that his children needed room in their lives to make their own choices and mistakes. He and his wife had one girl and two boys, Esther was the youngest. Earl loved his family dearly, but sometimes he took the stress from his job at a naval yard out on his family when he came home. The racist environment under which he had to work was very traumatic to his state of mind. The naval yard was located in Charlestown, an especially racist area of Boston. Earl had to be home by sundown or face the consequences of a bunch of cowardice white boys who thought they were tough using their baseball bats trying to

- 49 -

beat up on defenseless Black people at night on their way home from a long day's work. His wife was a homemaker, but she also moonlighted as a babysitter for a white family.

Esther was forced to quit school a few years earlier when the family fell on hard times. She had to get a job at the grocery store as a bagger to help alleviate the financial strain on the family when Earl lost his job as a janitor to a white man at Boston English High School. It took Earl two years to land his new job at the naval shipyard. Esther continued to work at the grocery store even after her dad got his new job. She wanted to continue to help contribute to the household. Her family had lost their apartment and was living in a rooming house for about six months, sharing one small room. They had to sneak around because the owner of the rooming house, who was a Jewish man, would not have allowed all of them to share the room. That experience brought the family even closer, so Esther vowed to never be without a job again. She wanted to always be in a position to help her family. Her mother worked as much as she could, but she was limited because she had two boys to raise at the time. After Earl secured a job, his plan was to save enough money to buy his own home in Roxbury. Though it was embarrassing to sneak around in this rooming house that they shared with other folks, it was well worth it because the family couldn't have saved the amount of money that they saved without that sacrifice. A Jewish banker whose family had had been victimized by the Holocaust helped Earl secure a loan at the bank. He sympathized with Earl and his family and he was able to get the loan approved without Earl ever showing up at the bank. The banker knew it would be a guaranteed denial if the bank knew that Earl was a black man. That same Jewish man helped a lot of other black families purchase homes, though the loans were at a higher interest rate. The family wanted to buy a two-family home in the heart of Roxbury, where the black community was striving.

The Jamison family wasn't shy about religion. Mrs. Jamison and her husband attended The First AME Baptist church every Sunday. It was something that most Black folks were doing back in the fifties and sixties. It was a way for them to make friends and congregate with other Black folks who migrated from all over the South to the North for better job opportunities. They believed in the word of God and they adhered to it. Esther was especially happy every Sunday because she looked forward to going to church. She enjoyed church more than the rest of her family. She was involved in many of the activities offered at the church, such as the young people's annual retreat, bible study, and anything that brought her to the church. Church was also one of the few places that she could go without her father creating a fuss.

Earl was a stand-up man who placed his family at the top of his list of priorities. He may not have had much, but he made sure he kept his family together. Even during the period when he was jobless, he decided to work as a day laborer. He would get picked up every morning in Roxbury and taken to different job sites where he was paid a measly five bucks a day for his hard work. The illegal Mexican immigrants are well-known modern day laborers, but Black folks did that when they first migrated North from the South. They were treated like foreigners in their own country. Being black back then was equivalent to being an illegal alien or worse. It seems as if America has always had its dirty little secrets in this so called "democracy." There has always been a trace of classicism in American society, which is almost equal to racism. The money Earl earned kept food on the table and provided for the family's basic necessities. The short stint that Earl's family had to do in the rooming house was through no fault of his own. After abruptly losing his job, he could only pay his rent for two months from his savings. His Jewish landlord was an impatient man who saw no solution to the problem, except to evict the family.

It was after that experience that Earl decided that he would own the next house that he'd move into, and would never jeopardize the well-being of his family again. The family worked tirelessly to save enough money for the down payment on a house. Earl worked odd jobs and waited until he landed his permanent job at the Naval Yard before buying his two-family home on Humboldt Street in Roxbury. It was the home where his boys would be raised, and his daughter would live with her future husband on the second floor until she and her husband bought their own house in Hyde Park.

Chapter 8
Courting Esther

Buck was as country as they come, and courting Esther was not something that he had on his agenda when he moved to Boston. The smile he received from Esther the very first time they met confirmed that she liked him and that's all he needed to know. They barely talked to each other before Buck decided to move to Boston. Esther wrote him a few times, but Buck was too embarrassed to respond. His sixth grade education wasn't enough for him to be able to write complete sentences and keep the communication lines open. Often times, he had to get his brother to read Esther's letters to him. He figured that all the hard work was done when he learned how much she liked him through her letters. However, Esther had been living up North since she was a child and they did things a little differently in the North. As far as Buck was concerned, Esther was already his woman and there was no need to woo her. Buck was far from romantic and he had no idea how to romance Esther.

Their usual outings were church, a movie, sometimes a bite to eat and nothing else. Buck was reserved and introverted, so he said very little when he and Esther got together. It was a drag to get him to utter more than three words at a time. Esther herself was a shy woman, but she had no problem expressing her feelings to Buck. As the relationship progressed, Buck did whatever Esther wanted and most of the time it was always the same routine. Even an evening stroll in downtown Boston was rare because Buck worked long hours. Overall, despite his social flaws, Buck was actually a likable guy and Esther found his six-foot-two-inch frame, dark chocolate skin, beautiful bright smile and chiseled face, appealing. Most of the time, Buck had a serious look on his face, but occasionally Esther would force a smile out of him with one of her witty comments, and he would melt her heart with his beautiful smile.

Buck found Esther to be a fascinating woman, and she saw Buck as an independent man who would be a good provider and caretaker. Back then, that was all that mattered, for two black people to develop a perceived loving relationship, anyway. Many black folks couldn't afford to do what white folks were doing. The family unit was the most important factor in a relationship and the church played a major role in that. Esther also admired the fact that Buck willingly moved to Boston to pursue her.

Buck wasn't the type of guy to bring her flowers or anything like that. In fact, he was pretty rigid. She honestly wanted more from a man, but the guilt of having him move all the way from New York to Boston got the best of her and she figured she could live with his flaws. Buck wasn't the best dresser when he first arrived to Boston. He would dress awkwardly with un-matching colors. However, with the help of Esther, he developed a better sense of style overtime. It wasn't like Esther was a fashionista herself, but she was a couple of steps ahead of Buck. She was proud of Buck and his hardworking habits, and her family absolutely loved him.

During the courting period, Buck would not allow Esther to even come to his room. He did not want to disrespect her in any kind of way. He wanted to cherish his girlfriend and treat her like a queen. He also did not want to fornicate before marriage, because his pastor had drilled in his head that fornication was forbidden. However, the pastor was fornicating with every attractive young woman in the church on the down low. Those women kept their mouths shut. He never tried anything with Esther because her father looked intimidating enough to break a foot in the pastor's ass. Buck admired his pastor and was grateful that Esther brought him to that church. After a year of courting Esther,

Buck had saved enough money to get his own apartment and felt that he was ready to marry her.

As rigid as he was, he couldn't figure out how to surprise Esther with an engagement ring, so he asked her to pick out her own ring. It was during the Christmas season and Esther's face was filled with glee. "You know you don't have to spend a lot of money on a ring for me. I don't care about that stuff," Esther said when they arrived at the jewelry store on Washington Street located downtown Boston. Buck was more interested in the decoration and the bright lights illuminating the streets of Boston. "I just want to make you happy. I know I ain't got too much right now, but I be working hard and we gonna buy us a house someday," he assured her. The idea of having a home, family and someone to love her, filled her heart with joy. The two of them walked the streets hand in hand after picking up her ring. Back then, black women especially didn't make a big deal of the bling in the ring. There was no time or money for that. Esther wanted Buck to ask her hand in marriage in front of her parents at the Christmas dinner where he was invited. She wanted it done that way because she did not want to show any kind of disrespect to her parents.

Esther wasn't even sure if she loved Buck when she agreed to marry him. It felt like the natural next step in their relationship after they had been dating for about a year. In the meantime, Buck was also getting heavily involved in the church. He and Esther went to church three to four times a week. The charismatic pastor in his church was becoming more likable than ever and his words became sacramental to Buck. Esther took notice in his desire as a Christian and she became fond of his endless search for the word of God.

The other character that Esther admired in Buck was the fact that he never tried to get physical with her. He never even as much tried to kiss her, unless she initiated it. Unlike those other hot boys who were always trying to get in her pants, Buck wanted to wait until they got married, before he got sexually involved with Esther. He truly lived by the word of the Bible. Esther herself was a virgin and was appreciative of the fact that she was not being pressured into doing anything. Kissing and necking with Buck was the extent of their physical contact and she did not push it further. The fear of her dad breaking one of his good feet up her ass and Buck's ass was also looming around in her head.

Chapter 9
Buck's New Family

It was a very festive Christmas in December the year 1969 for Buck. Though he missed his mother and wanted to spend the holiday with his family in upstate New York, the step he was about to take in his life was more important. It was going to be a new chapter in his life. Buck was excited about the idea of being married to Esther. He showed up at Esther's house at exactly six o'clock with gifts in hand for the whole family. Esther had helped pick out the gifts. He wasn't earning big money, so she took him down to Woolworth, which was a big department store at the time, to pick out items for each member of her family. Esther herself didn't want a gift from him because he had spent almost two hundred dollars on a ring for her. He bought her brothers each a shirt, a tie for her father and a beautiful apron for her mother; all were sales items. When Buck arrived at the house, everyone was waiting on him before starting dinner. After handing the gifts over to Esther, they headed to the dining room where the festive meal was taking place.

Dinner started with a prayer by Mrs. Jamison before everyone started digging into their plates. It was a normal meal, consisting of fried chicken, greens, macaroni and cheese, sweet potato pie, rice and cornbread. During dinner, the family got to know Buck a little more, but he was a little shy about answering all the questions. Whenever he was too shy to answer a question, Esther answered for him. The family welcomed him with open arms and Buck knew that he had to marry Esther. With the ring still in his right pants' pocket, Buck waited. Trying his best to overcome his shyness and his speech impediment, Buck stood up and asked for everybody's attention. Buck didn't so much have a speech impediment as he did a country accent. Coming from the Deep South had its disadvantage in a city like Boston. "Mr. and Mrs. Jamison, I be thinking about your daughter all day. I be smiling when I thinks about her and she be bringing joy to my heart," Buck said while everyone listened. "What are you trying to say, boy?" Mr. Jamison asked impatiently. "What I be trying to say is that I wants to marry Esther and I would like your approval, sir,' Buck stated with apprehension. When Mr. Jamison first met Buck, he thought he was a little too country for his daughter. However, Mrs. Jamison saw him for the kind southern man that he was and she asked her husband to give him a chance. Buck was hardworking and God fearing and that's really all that they ever wanted from him. "Now, it ain't really up to me whether my daughter will marry you or not, but I think it might be a good idea if you ask her too," Mr. Jamison said as he pointed Buck towards Esther.

Buck didn't really know the protocol for a proposal, but he soon got help from Mrs. Jamison as she told him, "You got to get on your knees to ask a woman to marry you, and you got to have a ring." Buck had completely forgotten about the ring in his pocket. He reached into his pants' pocket and got on both knees while he proceeded to ask Esther to marry him. However, Mr. Jamison chimed in and said, "You look like you're begging, boy. You ain't got to get on both knees to ask a woman to marry you." He moved towards his wife to demonstrate the gesture. Mrs. Jamison started blushing as her husband extended his hand to her hand and acted like he was about to propose to her all over again.   Buck went to follow the procedure and said to Esther, "I don't know the words to tell you how I feel, but I know that I wants to be with you for the rest of my life," as he placed the ring on her hand. No one in the room ever even noticed that Buck never told Esther that he loved her.

Buck was not accustomed to hearing those words from his own parents, so he grew up culminating the same attitude that his parents displayed towards each other. The lack of affection and emotion was natural to Buck. The mood was festive as the couple celebrated the engagement. A conversation about a wedding date ensued and Mr. Jamison wanted to make sure that his daughter had a decent wedding. Talks about renting the Skycap Plaza for the reception dominated the conversation all night. Buck was just happy and had no idea about what a wedding is supposed to be like. He had never been to one.

Chapter 10
Moving On

Buck and Esther were married at the First Baptist Church and the reception was held at the Skycap Plaza on Warren Street in Roxbury. Mr. Brown, the owner, gave them a deal on the place. BJ also gave Buck a generous wedding present of five hundred dollars. Buck's entire family drove to Boston for the wedding and his mother was so happy for him. Buck and Esther wasted no time getting pregnant after they got married. Katrina was conceived on the night of their honeymoon. It seemed as if two awkward people were making love and neither of them could evaluate each other's skills. They were both happy to finally get it on. Buck struggled at first to find the hole to insert his tool, but Esther was a little helpful as she used her finger, pointed and said, "I think that's it right there." Buck tried it once more and he was successful. However, Esther appeared as if she was in excruciating pain as Buck was less than gentle. The fact that he was well-endowed didn't help at all. Esther just laid there in pain and allowed Buck to do what he had to do. There was no broken hymen. Buck didn't have any suspicions because he didn't know much about the female body at the time. However, the worst part of it was the fact that she got pregnant on her first try.

Buck and Esther's bundle of joy arrived nine months later. The couple barely had any time to get to know each other well. Esther had to adjust to Buck's ways and he had to do the same. For the most part, she was a typical woman of the time. She cooked, clean and made sure her husband was taken care of. Buck also took on another job at the naval yard where Esther's dad worked. He was working two jobs to help support his family. They had also moved to the second floor apartment in Esther's father's house. Esther wanted to be as far away from her parents as possible, but her father insisted on the couple moving above them in order to help them save for their own home. At least that's what it appeared to be like. As much as Esther wanted to get away from her family by quickly marrying a man she barely knew, there was no escaping.

She was only eighteen years old when they got married. There was sadness on Esther's face most of the time, but she tried as much as she could to hide it. Something was tormenting her and she would keep it a secret for the rest of her life. She hoped, anyway. After her baby was born, Esther decided to devote herself to being the best mother possible. She named her daughter Katrina just because she liked the name. She watched over her child like a lioness, protecting her from everyone. Buck could hardly get anytime with his daughter without the presence of Esther. At first, Katrina would cry a lot when Buck would pick her up. There was never any attachment between the two. One day, Esther had to go to work and Buck had to watch Katrina for eight hours by himself. Katrina cried the whole time and Buck couldn't figure out why. He tried everything to make the baby comfortable, but Katrina wouldn't stop crying. It wasn't until Esther came home that the baby stopped crying.

Chapter 11
Esther's Demons

Before Katrina was born, Esther prayed that her child wouldn't come out with some kind of handicap or deformities. Buck would walk in the bedroom at night to find Esther on her knees praying to God with tears running down her face. He couldn't understand why his wife prayed and cried so much. "Baby, why you always be crying when you pray?" he asked one day. "I'm just thankful and praying that God give us a healthy baby," she answered. "Everything gonna be all right, baby. Our child will be just fine," Buck assured her. All of Buck's assurance couldn't ease Esther's mind. Her worries were deeper than anybody knew. Not even her mother knew what had been going on for years.

When Katrina was born, she looked like a normal baby, but favored her grandfather more than anybody. Through the years, she started to look more and more like her grandfather, which was a normal thing to Buck and the rest of the family. It's not unusual for a child to look like her grandparents. However, in Esther's case, Katrina looked exactly like her grandfather for a reason. From the time Esther was ten years old, when she started to develop breasts, the torment began. Her daddy would walk into her room and started fondling her for no reason. She knew what her father was doing was inappropriate, but she couldn't say anything. As time went on, he went from fondling, to kissing her. "You know I love you more than anything in the world, right baby girl? You can't tell anybody about this or you, your brother and your mommy will be living on the streets without daddy, ok?" her father would tell her. Esther would also be showered with gifts and spoiled by her father. Her mother admired the man who was so devoted to his daughter. Mr. Jamison always wanted to spend time with his daughter and her mother saw it as a beautiful thing. Even when Esther insisted that he bring her brothers along when they went on outings, he would tell his wife that he wanted to spend time alone with his little girl. One day during a trip to Franklin Park, Mr. Jamison took things farther than he had ever taken them before. Esther was barely twelve years old when he used his finger to break her hymen. There was no sympathy for the pain on Katrina's face as her dad forcefully took her virginity. The blood running between her legs was wiped with a dirty napkin her father found in his glove compartment. "You can't let nobody else touch you down there, but me," he said to her. She shook her head in agreement. Her virginity was lost and gone forever and from that day on, the incest began.

Mr. Jamison even changed his work schedule so he could be in the house alone with Esther when she got home from school. Esther was looking to be rescued, but she didn't know how to ask for help. The racist staff at her school didn't make themselves available or approachable to the black students. At the time, bussing was also a big issue in Boston. Esther had to deal with the racism at school, as well as the racist attitudes of the people in Boston on the street. Being raped by her dad daily was the least of her worries. After a while, Esther gave in to the "affection" that her father was bestowing upon her. Her father threatened to send her away if she ever told anybody and he would always profess his love for her as a source of comfort. As confusing as that sounds, Esther felt she had no choice. This arrangement went on even after she got married. Before marrying Buck, her father would never ejaculate inside of her. He would pull out each time. However, once she decided she was going to marry Buck, her father became jealous and wanted to make sure that their arrangement would last a lifetime. The week before the wedding, he had sex with her everyday without using protection. Esther already knew that there was a possibility that she was pregnant by her daddy, because of the morning sickness she was experiencing. Her only concern was that she may have a handicap child.

Esther managed to keep the sexual relationship with her dad from her husband for a while. Mr. Jamison would go upstairs to their apartment when Buck would be at work and he would continue to have sex with Esther. On Thanksgiving eve one year, Buck was told by his supervisor that he could leave work early to go be with his family. While walking through his house he could hear moaning and groaning coming from his room. At first, he thought his wife had another man in the house. The first thing he did was to go to the closet in the kitchen and grabbed a bat that he kept for protection. Buck was shocked to find Mr. Jamison and his wife naked in his bed having sex. There was sadness written on her face and he didn't know what to do. The only reaction was the swing of his bat across the back of Mr. Jamison. The beating continued until Mr. Jamison was knocked unconscious. "How long this been going on?" he asked his wife. With tears rolling down her face, Esther started to reveal to her husband the abuse she had been suffering at the hand of her father for many years. Buck was angry enough to kill Mr. Jamison, but he somehow managed to calm himself down and came up with a better solution. He wanted Mr. Jamison locked up for the rest of his natural life. Esther also wanted the same thing. She had so much hatred towards her father she could care less if he rotted in jail, but the raping had been going so long, she had gotten used to it.

She also thought about the consequences and the effect it would have on her mother and brothers. By the time Mr. Jamison woke up from his beating, Buck had decided that he would no longer be welcomed in his home. "I don't want you to ever set foot in this apartment for the rest of your natural life," Buck told Mr. Jamison while fuming. All Mr. Jamison could do was to shake his head in agreement as he hopped out of the apartment. He also wanted to keep it from the rest of the family, but Buck was too angry to allow that to happen. Figuring out what to do next was the big challenge for Buck and his wife. He hated living above a man who was cruel enough to rape his own daughter.

Buck tried as much as he could to convince his wife to report everything to the police, but she couldn't go through with it. She thought about her mother's ailing heart and the close relationship that her father had developed with her brothers. It would all be ruined. She was thinking about the greater good for her family even in agony and pain.

Esther also thought about all the times when her father showered her with gifts to keep her hushed. Honestly, Esther never wanted the gifts that her father gave her. His own guilt was the reason why he kept trying to buy her love. She was scared and confused, and for many years she would wrestle with the situation.

Buck was adamant about making sure that Mr. Jamison paid for his crime. However, before he could do anything about it, his number was called by Uncle Sam. The draft for the Vietnam War had just begun and Buck was required to serve one tour of duty. Two of his siblings were already in Vietnam and they had written to tell him to try to avoid the Army as much as he could. "We have no idea why we're fighting this war," one of his brothers wrote. "I don't know how we can hypocritically try to convert the whole world to democracy when it doesn't exist in our own country," wrote another brother. At first, Buck thought about running, but he would eventually be caught. So he decided to give Uncle Sam three years of his life, fighting a war that would leave him psychologically damaged for the rest of his life.

To top it off, Buck had a hard time finding a job when he came back from Vietnam. His strong belief in God and his discipline kept him from developing any bad habits while he was in Vietnam. After knocking on doors of different businesses for a few weeks without any luck when he came back from the war, Buck decided to become a day laborer so he didn't have to run through his savings. He would go stand on the corner of Blue Hill Avenue and Warren Street everyday at six o'clock in the morning waiting to be picked up by some white man who would offer him minimum wage to work as hard as a horse, so he could feed his family. There would be hundreds of black men waiting and fighting to get in the truck so they could have an opportunity to work. Finally, one day Buck got very lucky when this man who owned a construction company picked him up for work. He worked so hard that week for the man, the man decided to offer him a full-time job with his company.

The irony in Buck's situation when he came back from Vietnam was that his color or education wasn't an issue for the United States Army. He was able to join them and trained to become a killing machine for a country that didn't even want to give him the opportunity to feed his family because of the color of his skin and his lack of a high school education and college degree. He couldn't even get a job as janitor for a long time.

Chapter 12
ADVERSITIES

By the time Buck made it back home three years later, Katrina was already walking and talking. She was happy to see her dad make it home safe in one piece from Vietnam. Buck had also grown some balls while serving in Vietnam. When he came back home, he wanted nothing more than to move away from Esther's parents. Buck didn't write much while he was away, but he always made sure to tell his wife to try to do something about Mr. Jamison before he came back. By the fifth year in their marriage, Buck was growing resentful of his wife because she hadn't done anything about her father. She was happy that Buck was able to put a stop to the continuous rape, but now her husband was starting to feel like his wife actually enjoyed having sex with her dad. "That bastard father of yours belong in prison for the rest of his life," he would say to her whenever they got into an argument. She would never respond and he would continue, "Maybe you enjoyed it, is that why you don't wanna report it to the police?" Esther highly respected her husband, and she didn't want to talk back to him. This emotional abuse went on for awhile. The most tormenting part of it was the fact that she couldn't talk to anybody else about the situation. Her husband had grown so bitter; she thought her marriage would go down the tube.

Then there was the little girl named Katrina who looked just like Esther's father. DNA testing wasn't as prevalent then, but Buck had a hard time believing that Katrina was his daughter. His mind was just not at ease about the whole situation. He started to resent Katrina a little as well. His curiosity about the biological make-up of his daughter almost drove him insane, but he wasn't willing to spend the extra $400.00 at the time to pay for the blood test, which would prove paternity. Buck also felt ashamed about going to his family with the situation. He already knew how his brothers would feel about the situation because of the abuse they suffered at the hand of their own father. Rape would be punishable by death, if he ever told any of them. The only thing that Buck could do at the time was to pray about it and ask God to forgive his father-in-law.

Even the thought of going to see his pastor about the situation was not an option for Buck. His pastor often told his congregation to forgive and forget and Buck was especially influenced by the Bible. The charismatic pastor's translation of the good book made the words even more powerful. Buck started praying to God and asking for answers about his situation, but the answers didn't come as easy as he would have liked. The personal torment continued and his relationship with his child was affected. After the incident, Buck ceased all communication between his family and his father-in-law. He was cordial to his mother-in-law, but he never attended any Christmas, Thanksgiving dinners or any other special occasions at the Jamison's, ever. He would drag his wife to New York to spend time with his family. She couldn't dare say anything about him dragging her to New York because she knew her husband could've exploded at any time.

Esther's brothers felt that Buck was too controlling of their sister and they wondered if he was physically abusing her. They even offered to confront him if she was too afraid to do it. However, she assured them that Buck was the perfect gentleman; he just wasn't a people person. Buck had also changed churches. He started attending another Baptist church in Dorchester. He wanted all association with Mr. Jamison to end. Katrina also never spent any time at her grandmother's because of Mr. Jamison. Buck threatened to blow his lid if Esther ever let his daughter in the presence of Mr. Jamison. "I swear on the good Lord's name, if you ever let my child go downstairs to spend time with your mother and father, I will kill him," he told his wife. "What if my mother is around, she wants to spend time with Katrina too?" she rebutted. "Your mother was around the whole time your father was abusing you, she didn't do a damn thing about it, because she never could see it. That ain't happening to Katrina. I would kill your father first," he told her. The rage in Buck's voice was so real, Katrina was completely silent.

One can only imagine the rage that came out of Buck towards his wife the day that he came home to learn that his daughter was downstairs taking a bath in her father's apartment. For some reason, the hot water heater for the second floor broke earlier that day. Esther needed to give her daughter a bath, but there was no hot water. When Buck came home he was accustomed to his daughter running towards him for a warm hug every time. He couldn't find his daughter and Esther was nervous about telling him the truth, because of the crazy look on his face. "Where's Katrina?" he asked. Esther paused for a moment before deciding to answer. Buck's worse suspicion was about to be confirmed. "Where's my daughter?" he asked for a second time. "She's downstairs taking a shower because our hot water is out," she said rapidly as Buck made his way towards her. Something came over him and he wrapped his hand around her neck as he spewed, "I told you not to let my daughter around that child molester. I'm gonna kill you if something happens to her," he said angrily as he continued to choke her. Mrs. Jamison heard all of the commotion and started to make her way upstairs to Esther's apartment. When Mrs. Jamison entered the apartment she found Buck on top of Esther trying to choke the hell out of her. "Get off my daughter!" she screamed at the top of her lungs. Buck jumped back to catch himself. He didn't realize how badly he was hurting Esther. "What are you trying to kill my daughter!" her mother yelled at him. He couldn't respond. He walked towards his bedroom and closed the door.

Meanwhile, Katrina was left in the hallway behind the door while grandma checked on what was going. Katrina could hear their loud voices and she started shaking. She was sad that he father was hurting her mom. Buck walked back out of his room and said, "Go get my child!" to Mrs. Jamison. She quickly opened the door to let Katrina in. Buck grabbed his daughter and went to the bedroom. Katrina still had a towel wrapped around her body from taking a fresh bath and Buck looked her over to make sure everything was okay. He stepped back out of the room once more and said, "I don't ever want my child around that rapist ever again. If he as much as touch my child, I will kill him." He then walked back to his room without saying another word. Mrs. Jamison was baffled by his statement. She didn't know what the hell was going on and she wondered where Buck's rage was coming from. She had never seen that side of him before. "Esther, what is Buck talking about?" Mrs. Jamison asked as she held Esther's head in her arms. Esther never thought that it would come to that, but the moment of truth had arrived and she needed to find a way to tell her mother the truth.

With tears streaming down her face, Esther began to tell her mother the ordeal that her father had put her through since she was a little girl, "First, I need to tell you why Buck is so angry. He told me not to let Katrina downstairs after he found daddy raping me in my own bedroom. He had been touching me since I was a little girl. He made me do dirty things to him and he started having sex with me since I was twelve years old. I hate him and sometimes I wish Buck would kill him!" Her mother was shocked to hear the allegations. She wanted to say something but she was numb for a minute. It took a few minutes, but Mrs. Jamison was finally able to mutter a few surprising words to Esther. "You little hot pants Jezebel, my husband would never do such thing to you, and if he did, it's because your little too hot to trot behind was asking for it. I saw how you paraded around the house in your little shorts around my husband. Don't think that I don't notice the way you stare at me with jealousy and envy every time my husband is around. I don't even know why you think he's your father. I only allowed him to take you in because your parents were killed in a hit-and- run accident and nobody in your family would take you. He's not even your biological father, he's your godfather. I know you didn't know this, but my husband has had pity on you since you came to live with us as a baby girl, and for you to sit there and blame him for something he did not do...you're nothing but an ingrate," she told Esther. For the first time in her life, Esther finally confirmed the suspicions that she was not biologically Mr. Jamison's daughter even though people thought they resembled each other. The two boys were the spitting image of their mom and dad, Esther looked totally different. Mrs. Jamison couldn't keep her mouth and emotion separate that evening.

Mrs. Jamison always resented the fact that her husband wanted to take on the responsibility of raising Esther. They already had the two boys when she came to live with them as a baby, but Mr. Jamison desperately wanted a girl with his wife. One Sunday afternoon while

Esther's parents were on their way to church, a car careened out of control, jumped the curb and ran over them. Her dad was able to push the baby carriage out of the way just in the nick of time to save Esther. She lost both parents that morning and the white drunk driver was never caught. Since no one from Esther's biological family wanted to adopt her, Mr. Jamison talked his wife into taking her in. At the time, he and Esther's dad were best friend and also Esther's godfather. Mr. Jamison and his wife decided that they would raise Esther as their own child, but the resentment started soon after Mr. Jamison lost his first job. It took him a while to land on his feet, but he would lose his job again later on in life. Instead of asking the two older boys to help with the household finances, Esther was forced to quit school and join the workforce. As a child, she never questioned her parents' decisions. The fact that she was being sexually abused also forced her to be docile and passive. Esther had been passive for so long, it was a matter of time before she blew up.

As rage boiled up inside Esther, Mrs. Jamison knew the wrath was coming from the stare in Esther's eyes. "Get the hell outta my house! I don't ever wanna see yo face no mo. I hate you!" Mrs. Jamison had a smirk on her face before Buck walked out of the room and forcefully said,

"You heard her, get the hell out!" He heard everything that Mrs. Jamison said to his wife, and he was more sympathetic than ever. Buck realized that his wife was at their mercy her entire life and he became her savior.

Something else dawned on Esther after Mrs. Jamison left the apartment. Her whole life she had been treated like a stepchild by Mrs. Jamison and she couldn't understand why. She was always the person to clean the house, cook for everyone, do the laundry and every other chore needed in that house. She was also the one who was forced to quit school so she could go to work and help with the household bills. Everything suddenly made sense to her. She came to live with the Jamisons when she was a few months old and the Jamisons promised that they would never tell her that she was not their biological child. Mrs. Jamison crossed that line in defense of her husband, and from that day on, the relationship between them and Esther was nonexistent.

Chapter 13
Family Secrets

After the incident with Mrs. Jamison, things would never be the same again with the Jamison family. Mr. Jamison denied the whole incident ever took place and he made his wife believe that Esther and Buck were conniving liars. Of course, he would never face Buck and Esther when he made his claims, but Mrs. Jamison bought the story he told her. "I can't believe that little tramp had the nerve to say such bad things about you. And her country bumpkin husband was there standing next to her lying through his teeth too. I think I know what this is about. They probably don't want to pay us rent anymore," she said. "You're right honey, that's probably what it is. It ain't like they been paying on time the past few months anyway," he said to her. Mrs. Jamison's gullible behind was standing there taking it all in. Buck was a man of principle and the one thing he would never do was to not pay his rent on time. Mr. Jamison had been lying to his wife about getting the rent late from Buck because he had a gambling, as well as a sexual addiction. Often times, he lost the rent money shooting craps or spent it on the prostitutes in the local brothels in Roxbury. He would rely on his luck to earn the money back while shooting craps.

Meanwhile, Esther's brothers had no idea what was going on. Mr. and Mrs. Jamison were trying their best to keep everything from them, but Junior would inevitably run into Esther one day while she was on her way upstairs to her apartment. Mr. Jamison named his first son after him. "What's going on, sis? How come you don't come downstairs no more to see us, said the eldest of the two boys when he saw her. "Junior, I been busy with Katrina and I ain't had time to come down. I don't think I'll be coming down there too much no more, anyway." "Why not? You ain't just gonna stop seeing your family cause you got married, right?" "That's not it, Junior. I just have a lot more to do now," she told him. "You know something, sis? I don't know if I like your husband too much. He done changed you ever since y'all got married. You seem like a stranger, like you ain't even our sister no more," he said with sadness in his voice. Esther could sense the innocence in her brother's voice. She walked towards him and gave him a hug. She fought back tears as she told her brother, "I love you Junior. I love all of you and I wish things could be different, but I gotta go cause my husband is upstairs waiting for me to get home so he can go to work."

Esther knew that she and Buck were gonna have to move quickly out of that apartment, because she wanted to protect her relationship with her brothers. She also wanted to shield them from everything that was going on. Growing up, Esther only knew one family. She was at a crossroad after Mrs. Jamison revealed that she was not biologically part of the family. She was now questioning who she really was. She was also relieved to know that she was not walking around carrying any traits of Mr. Jamison in her. However, that was not the case for her daughter. That rapist was her father and she knew it. It was no wonder Katrina was not born with any kind of deformities, there was no biological link between Esther and Mr. Jamison.

Chapter 14
Moving Ahead

Five years after Katrina was born, Buck and Esther welcomed their son, Eddy, to the world. Buck couldn't stand the sight of Mr. and Mrs. Jamison and he knew he had to get out fast and in a hurry. He was smart enough to save most of the money that his brother gave him in addition to his personal savings from his job. He had close to three thousand dollars saved, which was more than enough for the house he wanted to purchase in Hyde Park, Massachusetts, which bordered Mattapan. The bank required a twenty percent deposit in order for Buck and Esther to get approved for the loan, but more importantly, they asked for an additional cosigner. Buck saw these things as nothing more than obstacles he could overcome. The house was only twenty thousand dollars and he had more than enough money for the down payment. Other than racism, there was no reason to require a cosigner. Buck made more than enough money from his two jobs to pay the monthly mortgage, even at an inflatable rate. Buck had always been an independent person and he wanted to do things on his own. However, his moving from the Jamison household needed to be expedited and he had to put his pride aside and ask his brother BJ to cosign for his loan. After explaining his situation to BJ, the seventeen thousand dollars he needed was wired to him in three days. BJ set up a payment plan where Buck had to pay him back half the amount the bank requested. He paid for the house in full and the white people selling it to him were shocked that he was able to come up with that kind of money.

Back in the seventies in Boston, banks and neighborhood associations worked together to make sure they kept black people out of certain neighborhoods. Even if BJ had decided to cosign the loan for Buck, they would have still found a reason not to sell the house to him because he was black. The street where Buck bought his house was made up of mostly white residents who harassed him and his family from the day he moved in. The white sellers were threatened daily right up to the day they vacated the house. One of the reasons they decided to sell to Buck was because they needed the money to help care for their son who was suffering from Leukemia. In their heart-of-hearts, they probably wouldn't have sold that house to a black man, but the cash transaction expedited the process and their hearts were filled with hope for their son. Buck had finally gained the independence he was searching for when he moved into his own house in Hyde Park with his family.

"We don't want your kind in our neighborhood," they would tell Buck as he made his way to work in the morning. He used to have flashbacks about white people chasing him and his brothers all over when he was growing up in the South. He decided he wasn't going to be chased anymore. He bought a shotgun and made it known to his neighbors if any of them ever set foot on his property to leave any kind of racially charged notes on his door, he would shoot to kill. Buck had been running all his life and he knew if he didn't start standing up for himself, and now his family, he would continue to run for the rest of his life. Often times, Buck really didn't know what to do, because he knew that he didn't want to shoot any of the white folks harassing him. Prayer became a huge part of his life, and his dedication to God took precedence over everything.

As time went on, Buck started to get more and more into religion and the church. The more he started to understand the Bible, the more forgiving he became. However, he had a hard time reading the scriptures due to his lack of education. Esther was a little more educated, but she was no scholar. Buck tried his best to hide his illiteracy from his wife, but his hunger for the word of God was voracious. He would have his wife read different psalms to him everyday before he left the house and every night before he went to bed. Buck often blamed his inability to read on poor eyesight, which was a convenient lie at the time. However, Esther was able to figure out that Buck was not a better reader than she was, and she didn't want to embarrass her husband. She wanted to keep his pride intact, so she never even made it an issue. Over time, Buck was able to forgive the ordeal with Mr. Jamison, but he couldn't forget.

Buck and Esther would welcome their third child, Karen, into their new home twenty months after moving in. He took on a second job again while his wife stayed home with the kids. Once his brother offered to give him the money for the house, he had quit his second job, but when Karen came he had no choice. He worked his full-time job from 7:00 AM to 3:00 PM and worked as an apprentice to a plumber at his church in the afternoon. Buck came home feeling tired everyday, but his girls and son would always bring a smile to his face. He would always make time for them before he went to bed. He loved his wife dearly, but he didn't always know how to express that love, and neither did she. Having been accustomed to no affection while growing up, didn't prepare Buck and Esther for parenthood.

As long as he provided for his family, that was enough love. Esther, however, became the more loving parent and started to show more affection towards the children. She would give the world for her husband. He took great care of her and made sure that they never went without. The family was finally complete. Buck got everything that he always wanted.

He worked tirelessly and relentlessly to try to pay the loan back to his brother BJ. Buck understood that his brother had always been there for him and he wanted to make sure he kept his promise to his brother. He tried as much as he could to stay in touch with his brothers, sisters and his mother, but as his family grew, he had less time to travel to New York to see them. Working two jobs also became a time constraint, but Buck's goal would not be denied. His highest monthly expenditure was the loan for the house, and he wanted to pay it off within a five-year period. He sacrificed buying a car and other luxuries so he could reach his goal. Esther was always supportive and she never once complained about taking the bus everywhere with the three children. Buck knew that he needed to buy a car for the family and he was making plans to do so as soon as he finished paying off his home. However, there were some other barriers to Buck having a car. Studying for the learner's permit required a certain level of reading ability that Buck lacked. He was trying to figure a way around it, but he couldn't. He knew that he didn't want to go through life having to take the bus everywhere, so he suggested that his wife got her license first.

Chapter 15
Navigating Through Life

Esther was able to secure a learner's permit after successfully passing the written exam. Buck paid a driving school company to teach his wife how to drive and soon she was able to get her license. After getting her license, Buck was able to buy Esther a used car for $300.00 from a co-worker. It took some sacrifice, but he was able to do it. Esther no longer had to worry about taking the bus, but with three kids, she was no longer able to work her part time job. Buck decided that his wife should be a housewife. He held two full-time jobs to help secure the financial future of his family. Things got a little easier as Esther was able to drop him off, to and from, work. She would have the kids in the back while she took her husband to work.

Over time, Esther needed a break from the children, but there was no relief in sight. With no extended family to depend on, she resigned with the fact that they were her children and she had to do what she to do to care for them. Since Buck spent sixteen hours of his day at the two jobs he held down, he had very little time to help with the children.

However, on his day off he would take his family on outings at the park. He especially liked the drive-in movies because it was more economical.

Without realizing it, Esther went through post partum depression after giving birth to her daughter Karen. Her mood swings were awful and there were times when she felt like hurting her daughter. She would lock her in a room by herself when she would cry, while she tried as best as she could to cope with the situation. She kept the mood swings hidden from her husband because he was not supportive when she complained. "I need a little break from these children. I need some time alone before I lose my mind," she once told her husband. He became irate and started yelling at her, "How the hell do you think I feel everyday, huh? I gots to go out there and work two jobs to help put a roof over your head and food on the table, but I ain't complaining because I gots to do what I gots to do. Your only job is to take care of the kids and you always whining about it." Esther knew then that she could never ask her husband to watch the kids so she could have a break. Her husband had no idea how difficult it was to care for three young kids everyday. Since the children were only a few years apart, Esther wouldn't get a break until Katrina, the oldest child, started school. She could've easily gone crazy during those first six years. It was a miracle how she managed to maintain her sanity while caring for three children with very different personalities.

Karen was especially difficult as she was the sneakiest of the three children. She would always find something to get into and Esther had to keep an eye on her all the time.   Since the family couldn't afford to buy a television at the time, children's programming on TV was out of the question. Esther had to find ways to entertain the kids. Buck also expected a warm meal everyday, as well as a clean house and clean clothes. It was like Esther basically held down two full-time jobs herself as she tried to accomplish these tasks everyday. However, Buck had no idea how difficult her days were and he would never know because he never wanted to take over her duties, even for one day.

Chapter 16
The Drama Unfolds

After a few years, and through conversation with her oldest brother, Esther was able to reveal to him why her relationship with the family had deteriorated. For a long time they had only heard Mr. and Mrs. Jamison's version. Her other brother showed solidarity and believed every word that his parents told him about Esther. He felt like she owed his parents gratitude because they took care of her, but Junior was always more reluctant and he continued to call his sister occasionally. She had been his sister all his life and he didn't know how to stop being a brother to her like his younger brother. His heart was in a different place. Often times, they both would opt out of talking about the family. They would just kick it on the phone as brothers and sisters do.

Junior had since gotten married and had a family of his own, a daughter and a son. His daughter was five years old and his son was three years old. Unfortunately, Junior found out the hard way how real Esther's situation with her dad had been. One day while giving his daughter a bath, she pointed to his crotch and said, "Daddy's wee wee. I wanna play with it." He couldn't figure out where she had learned such a thing, so he asked his wife. His wife couldn't confirm that she had talked to their daughter about a "wee wee," much less playing with one. At the time, Junior didn't want to entertain the conversation with his daughter so he let the sleeping dog lay. But, the deviant inquiry from his daughter continued, even when he was just sitting on the couch with her. She even reached for his crotch one day and he went off on her and told her not to ever do that again. His daughter's inquisitive mind was driving him crazy. He couldn't understand how a child so young was constantly making references to his sexual anatomy. Junior and his wife went to their daughter's school to find out if she had possibly learned these bad things from the other students at school, but to no avail. The teacher assured them that it wasn't at the school. The teacher even informed them that she was planning on having a meeting with them to discuss his daughter's sudden sexual approach to the young boys at the school.

Junior's children's overnight visits to their grandparents' home were the norm. Junior and his wife especially enjoyed the quality time together while the children were away. They savored those moments, as they got to be foolish with each other and take a breather from the kids. It never crossed their mind that they were putting their children in harm's way. Junior never even bothered to discuss Esther's allegations of rape against his father with his wife. It was a non-issue. At first, he believed that his father wouldn't cross the line with his sister. One thing that stood out to him was the fact that, until the incident, his parents never bothered to mention that Esther was adopted. He always wondered why she looked so different in complexion and physical beauty, but he didn't question whether or not she was his sister. The only person with a darker complexion in the family and kinky hair, Esther looked nothing like her fair skin, curly haired brothers who looked much like their mother and father. While Junior's mother pushed for him to sever ties with his sister, Junior wanted to make his own decision. Though their conversations were brief in the beginning, over time, Junior was able to reconnect with his sister as long as they didn't discuss the family problems.

Junior's bond with Esther was rekindled especially after he found out that his dad was molesting his own daughter. Little Malika was the happiest little girl until her grandfather started down the path of destruction with her. She started acting out at school and even started playing with matches at home, which is a sign of sexual abuse. The day that she told her dad that her grandfather had been forcing her to play with his penis, was the day that Junior lost it. He went to Mr. Jamison's house with the intent to kill him. With a loaded .38 revolver tucked in his waist, Junior impatiently drove to his parents' house. The sweat beads forming on his brow as he put the pedal to the metal was enough proof that it was time to kill. Then tears started rolling down Junior's cheeks as he started blaming himself for putting his daughter in harm's way. He didn't even bother checking the facts with Esther's case because he didn't believe that his own father could be such an animal.

As he pulled into the driveway, he pulled the gun from his waist to double-check and make sure that the gun was fully loaded. He placed it back on his waist, pulled his shirt over his pants and walked up to the door. He didn't bother ringing the door bell, as he banged as hard as he could on it with his fist. When his mother answered the door, she knew something was wrong. Junior had this devilish, deadly look in his eyes. "Junior, what's the matter with you, why are you trying to break down my door? You got better home training than that!" she said to him. "Where's daddy?" he asked angrily. "Your daddy is upstairs in the bedroom. What's the matter?" she asked. Junior didn't even bother giving his mother an answer as he rushed up the stairs to go find his father. He rushed through the door, pulled his gun and opened fire. By the time the shooting stopped, the gun was empty and there was a bloody mess on the bed. Mr. Jamison was on the bed jerking off to pictures of little girls when his son caught him off guard.

Mr. Jamison had been purchasing pictures of young girls illegally from a catalog without his wife's knowledge. Junior would not have to explain anything because his father had left the proof by his side on the bed. Mrs. Jamison came running upstairs to find a shaken Junior on the floor with the gun in his hand while tears flooded his face. Mrs. Jamison was hysterical at first, thinking that Junior had shot her husband for no reason. "What did you do, Junior?" she asked with her eyes filled with anger. "He was molesting Malika, momma," he said through sobs. "Why would you say something like that, Junior?" she asked with sadness in her voice. "She told me, momma. We should've reported him years ago when we learned he was doing it to Esther," he told her. Mrs. Jamison came to her husband's defense and suddenly was in attack mode against her son. "I would not let you dishonor your father like this. He was an honorable man. That little tramp was lying!" she said angrily as she slapped her son. "Momma, when are you gonna start believing that daddy wasn't so perfect? He managed to fool all of us, and now my daughter has to suffer the consequences. You need to stop being so delusional, momma." She rushed towards him and started swinging at him, hitting him all over. He tried holding her to calm her down while attempting to comfort her with a hug.

As Mrs. Jamison sobbed over her son's shoulder, she noticed the pictures of the young naked girls spread all over the bed. "We can't let the cops find him like this," she told her son. She ran towards the bed to pick up the pictures before the cops arrived, but Junior wouldn't let her. "No momma. They have to see him for the man he truly was, momma. He was a monster and he made life hell for others. Just leave him be, momma," he said while holding her.

Moments later, the cops arrived at the scene. They questioned Junior and his mom about the incident. He willingly gave the cops a true account of what happened. He was placed under arrest and read his rights. Junior was taken down to the precinct and booked for second degree murder. The case managed to make the papers and a prominent lawyer offered his services pro bono to help defend Junior. The lawyer was able to argue in court that Junior was defending his daughter and bail was set at a thousand dollars. He was able to walk out of prison because his employer posted bond for him. Junior was a dedicated worker at the Gillette Company, where he had been working for many years. He was well liked by his co-workers and managers. They were able to pull together the money to get him out. The whole city sympathized with him and they understood how hard it must've been for him to stand up to his father.

It was just the beginning of the story behind the predator. Mr. Jamison had been molesting kids in his path everywhere he went. There were victims at his church, in the neighborhood, and even his own kids' friends. The man was sadistic and a maniac. There were victims as old as Esther and as young as four years old. The judge in the case had no choice but to let Junior walk because of the outpouring of support for his actions. It was the first time that black and white people had come together to defend a black man accused of murder.

The case also created a wedge between Junior and his younger brother, Tommy, who felt that Junior had no right to kill their father. He didn't understand the emotion that overcame Junior when he found out his little princess was molested. Tommy hadn't yet gotten married or become a parent. Even with the insurmountable evidence that his father left behind after a thorough search of his house through a warrant, he didn't want to go against his dad. Mrs. Jamison was caught in the middle between the two sons. She knew that her husband was wrong for having done what he did, but she didn't want him gone. Nobody wanted him gone, not even Junior. However, there were some feelings he just couldn't fight. For a while Junior felt bad about taking his father's life and he wished he had thought the whole thing through better. He wished his dad had been the model grandfather to his daughter that every kid wishes to have, but that wasn't the case. He even had nightmares continuously about the ordeal.

Chapter 17
Mixed Emotions

Everybody in the family had mixed emotions about the death of Mr. Jamison. Some people were relieved that he was no longer around to torment young children, while others wished he paid for his crime behind bars for the rest of his life. Esther was especially distraught because she never knew that she could hate a person so much and love him at the same time. While Mr. Jamison took advantage of her as a little girl, he also played the role of daddy in her life. They shared some good times, which were overshadowed by the bad times. Most of her life she had wished that he would disappear from the earth. And when he was finally gone, she didn't have that feeling of satisfaction she yearned for. Esther was now tormented by her own inner hatred for her dad. She thought that she may have talked up his death. Maybe if she had learned to suppress those feelings, he would still be alive.

The funeral was emotional for most people in the family. Many of the distant family members worried that their children could've been victimized by Mr. Jamison.

Their children spent nights over Mr. Jamison's house at slumber parties. They showed up at the funeral to pay their respects, but in a way, most of them wished they had stayed home. There was almost no reason to celebrate a man that was such a monster to kids. However, Mr. Jamison was also a pillar in his community. During the holiday seasons, he would help feed the homeless, looked out for the families on his block when times were hard, even when he was dealing with hard times himself. He coached the little league football team, voluntarily. The little boys looked up to him and the people at his church respected him.

Tommy and his dad were especially close because they shared the love of football. They would sit together on the couch all day on Sundays at the house to watch the games while Mrs. Jamison cooked. Tommy also made his father proud by excelling on the football field in high school. Mr. Jamison never missed any of his son's games. Tommy's relationship with his dad was very personal. He tried as much as he could to please his dad. Junior, however, was a little more outgoing and involved with his friends. Instead of watching the games, he would be outside playing football with his buddies. He loved his father as any son would, but he cherished his mother even more. He liked the fact that his mother was dedicated to the family and loved her husband.

Of course, tears were shed, but there was also contempt at the funeral. Buck didn't bother showing up because he didn't want to see the man's face another time. Esther was all alone until Junior reached out to bring her into the family circle. She looked like a confused child as she wrestled with her emotions towards her dad. Sadness, anger, pain, delusion, confusion and restlessness took over her mind, body and spirit. The only family she felt she had left was her husband and children.

Though Mrs. Jamison felt bad for scolding Esther and calling her a tramp, she was too small of a person to apologize. Esther took the high road and offered her a hug when she needed consoling. The two women hugged like nothing was wrong between them as they mourned the, once special, man in their lives.

Chapter 18
A Brutal Reality

After Mr. Jamison died, Esther pretty much cut all ties with her family. She spoke on the phone occasionally with her brother, Junior, but that was far and between. Her focus shifted to her own family. Her husband was no easier on her as he expected everything from a wife and more. He was the provider and she was the mother of his children, his housekeeper, his harlot and nothing more. Buck was far from sensual, affectionate and supportive. He didn't know how to be any of those things because he had never experienced or witnessed any of it throughout his life. At times, he seemed overly crude to his wife and he acted like a brute in the bedroom, most of the time.

Esther did her duties as a wife when Buck wanted to have sex, but she never received any pleasure from it. Though Buck was not a drinker, he was the meanest son of a bitch to his wife for no reason at all, sometimes. At night, after putting the kids to bed, Esther would get in bed with her husband without saying much to him. There was no open communication between the couple. She would face one side of the room while he faced the other. It was a cold household and they didn't know how to talk to each other. When Buck wanted to have sex, he would simply roll over and try to penetrate his wife without touching or kissing her. She didn't dare ask him to be gentle with her because it would undermine him as a man. She would lie on the bed like a stiff board and allow her husband to have his pleasure. The look on Esther's face was almost similar to the reaction she would have when her father was raping her. It had become the norm to her and she simply tried to cope with it. Esther never had the chance to experience sexual stimulation because Buck had stopped caressing and kissing his wife months after they got married. That was the very little of it he did, then.

Buck also had a hard time expressing himself to his wife because he just didn't know how to do it. All he knew was that providing for his family made him the man of the house, and his desires had to be fulfilled, his needs met and his rules followed. Esther had become the submissive, domesticated wife that Buck desired. She relied on him for everything and he made sure he kept it that way for a long time. Life for Esther was hell as she knew it, but she was committed to her marriage and her family. Besides, she had nowhere to run to if she left.

Buck didn't make things any easier when he got home from a bad day at work. Everyone felt his wrath, including the children. Though he wasn't physically abusive to his wife, his kids suffered the brunt of his abuse. Every little thing would set him off and he would fly of the handle at home. Having to deal with racism at his job on a daily basis was taking its toll on Buck, but he couldn't leave his job because it was the best job he could've found as a black man without an education at the time. His white co-workers would make racist comments that made him feel like he was less than a man and Buck didn't know how to react to it.

One day a white liberal co-worker advised him to report the abuse to his boss, but his complaints went unanswered. His boss was the most racist of them all. He was trying his best to get rid of Buck, who was probably the most efficient and best worker on the assembly line, but he couldn't. Buck's record at work was spotless. He had never been late and had never done anything to jeopardize the livelihood of his family at work. However, one day one of his co-workers went too far. Buck was coming out of the bathroom one day when one of his white co-workers said to him, "I wish you niggers had your own bathroom here, because good white men like myself shouldn't have to take a dump where you niggers should eat." It took but a second for Buck to process the white man's comments and it took even less time for Buck to lay him out flat on his back with a punch to the jaw. Of course, Buck was suspended without pay for two weeks and if any other similar incident took place at work, he would be fired. To make matters worse, the white boy filed a criminal complaint and Buck was arrested.

While at the police precinct in Boston, Buck was denigrated by the white police officers. He was also threatened with a beating for having knocked out a white boy. However, they were cautious because they had heard about Buck's vicious right hand. Buck spent a few days in jail before a liberal judge threw the case out of court. He was lucky. He returned to work to an even more volatile environment. His victim threatened to get him back, but Buck wasn't fazed. There were times when a truck load of white boys would show up at his job and make empty threats to him, but they feared that he would take a few of them out. Buck was a pretty big and intimidating looking guy, so the white boys kept their distance. He made it clear to them that he would protect himself and his family. Buck feared that the cowardice white boys may one day attack his wife while she was picking him up, so he decided to quit his job for his family's safety. That decision brought on even more problems at home.

Buck had gotten his plumbing license by then, but he wasn't making enough money to pay all the bills with that one job. There weren't too many home owning black folks in Boston who needed plumbing work done that Buck could keep as clients to help support his family. He caught a lucky break when a fellow church member mentioned a job opening with the City of Boston. Buck was able to use the man as a reference and he was hired by the City of Boston's Water and Sewer Department. There, Buck would endure even more malice, racism and hatred. His friend had warned him about the hostile environment, but Buck had no idea how hostile it was going to be. This time Buck wouldn't allow anybody to run him from his job. Though he was qualified for the job, some of the white men felt slighted because another black man was hired to work along with them. Buck was paid much less than his white counterparts, but did a much better job than they did. He would go on to work for the City of Boston until he retired.

Chapter 19
Legal Limbo

Black people would go on to adopt the same method of discipline that was used against them many years ago to make them docile, against their children, capital punishment. Having been raised by a father who only knew one way to discipline his children, Buck became familiar with the violent leather belt strap that kept him in line as a child. His father was an overly boisterous man who ruled with an iron fist, which ultimately led to his death. Though Buck loathed his father's ways, after he had children, he couldn't break the cycle. His inability to verbalize to his family his torment at work and his daily struggles in a world designed to keep him in his "place," started to take a toll on his family.

Buck would lash out violently against his children, and as a result, the severe beatings the children received from him would leave bruises all over their bodies. There was one particular incident where Katrina missed her school bus and she didn't know how to get home. Her parents waited until it was dark and she still hadn't gotten home. By the time a police officer brought her home, it was almost nine o'clock at night. Buck was fuming and didn't understand why she didn't just pick up the phone to say she was lost. Katrina wasn't just lost, she had also gone over a friend's house and she lost track of time. After the police officer left, Katrina received the beating of her life. At ten years old, her father beat her like she was a grown woman. When she arrived at school the next day, the teacher could sense the discomfort in her body language. Curious to know why Katrina was so fidgety in class, the teacher started to inspect her covered arms. The inspection revealed a grossly bruised Katrina. The Department of Social Services was called and an investigation of child abuse ensued.

Buck's family was taught a way to discipline long ago, and those same teachings threatened the very existence of his family. The Department of Social Services' investigators soon invaded the Johnson family home, and Buck and Esther found themselves subjected to intimidation by the state. Katrina was immediately removed from the home and placed in a foster home with another family until the investigation was complete. There was no denying that Buck had beaten the crap out of his daughter because of the evident bruises, but it didn't mean that he didn't love his child. Though sympathetic because she was also black, the case worker had to follow the procedures according to state guidelines in order to ensure the safety of Katrina.

Katrina's bruises were so bad that the state considered filing criminal charges against Buck and his wife. Even though the other two children weren't part of the investigation, they were also removed as a precaution. The home front would never be the same as Esther blamed her husband for her children being taken away by the state. She would plead with him to ease up on raising his hands on the kids, but he would get angry at her and thought she was undermining him as a father. She knew her husband was cruel at times, but there was nothing that she could do to prevent any of it. Karen and Eddy would remain in foster care for three months before the state made the decision to return them home. Buck and Esther had supervised visitation with the kids while they were in foster care. They also had to enroll in parenting classes where they learned to deal with their frustration. It was a joyful day when Karen and Eddy were returned to their parents, but Esther was still sad because Katrina was still in foster care.

Chapter 20
Worse Than Home

Had Katrina known better, she would've acted like nothing was wrong with her at school on the day that her teacher discovered her bruises. Foster care turned out to be a nightmare. Due to the lack of homes for foster children, the State of Massachusetts approved a lot of people as foster parents that should have been red flagged. One family in particular was the Chaney family. Most people who decide to become foster parents usually do it out of the kindness of their hearts to help children. However, the Chaneys saw it as an opportunity to make extra money. The three-bedroom home they owned was converted to a mini hotel for adolescents. Each room was equipped with two double beds, including an additional two bedrooms in the basement. They could house a total number of sixteen children in their home, which the state should have deemed illegal. But due to the lack of homes for black children, the Chaneys were allowed more than their share of kids, especially in emergency situations. It may not sound like a lot of money, but sixteen children at an average of five hundred dollars each a month is a total of eight thousand dollars a month, plus an additional clothing allowance of one hundred dollars per child.

No foster parent should be able to get rich off this money if they're taking proper care of their foster children. However, the Chaneys spent very little money on food and clothing for their foster children. The children's daily meals consisted of hot dogs, beans, generic cereal, ramen noodles, government cheese, powder milk, fat back, spam, bologna, rice, grits, chicken liver and turnips. The Chaneys barely spent one hundred dollars a week on groceries. The boys took baths three at a time and the girls had to do the same. Mr. and Mrs. Chaney cared more about the green than they cared about the children. Neither of them worked because Mr. Chaney used his disability to supplement his income. He drove a brand new Cadillac while his wife drove a sixteen-passenger van. The only recreational activity the children enjoyed was the free ride to Franklin Park and the occasional cook-out in the back yard during the summer. In the winter time, the children stayed in the house and all lights had to be out by eight o'clock. Mr. Chaney hated having his electricity bill exceed sixty dollars a month. The thermostat for the heat was also set at the minimum sixty five degrees no matter how cold it was outside.

Katrina's adjustment to this new place was hell and she couldn't wait to get back to her parents' house. It was this experience that shaped her views about the foster care system. She would avoid having her kids placed in foster homes at all cost in the future. Katrina also didn't get along with the other children in the home. There were times when she went to bed hungry because the other children had eaten all the food by the time she got home from school. Food was served on a first-come first-serve basis at the house. Mrs. Chaney would make a pot of food, she thought was big enough to feed all the children, but it was never enough. Katrina wasn't the only child who felt slighted at the home. Many of the other children felt the same way, but they didn't come from a fortunate situation like Katrina did.

Most of the other children in the home came from drug addicted parents who were either on the street or locked up in jail. Many of them were crack babies with complications that scared most of the foster parents in the system. One of the reasons the Chaneys were given so much leeway was because they were one of a few foster families who took in the crack babies and other children with diagnoses such as, attention deficit disorder, lead poisoning, bipolar disorder, schizophrenia and other behavioral issues.

The more severe the diagnosis, the more money they received for that child and the more care and attention that child needed. Whether or not the children received the necessary care and attention depended on the actual number of visits the case worker made to the home. Due to case overloads, the case workers barely made more than one visit to the home and each visit was announced, which gave Mr. and Mrs. Chaney plenty of time to make things appear as well as possible.

It was time to get outta dodge and Katrina didn't want to spend another day at the Chaney home. Mr. Chaney was a mean son of a gun who didn't have to say much to enforce his rules. The killer look in his bloodshot red eyes was enough to scare the pants off the kids. There was no talking back or the consequences were harsh. Though these kids had been placed with the Chaneys because of abuse in their own home, there appeared to be a lot more potential of abuse in the Chaney home due to the overcrowding. Mr. and Mrs. Chaney somehow managed to go under the radar for many years as the destitute children felt there was no place else to go if they left the hell they were in. Katrina wasn't so destitute and she knew she had a mother who loved her dearly. She would keep calling her social worker and ask to be returned home to her parents.

A few months after Mr. and Mrs. Johnson completed their parenting classes, a hearing was held in family court in Boston and they were granted custody of their daughter. The court agreed to allow Katrina to go back home, but the visits by the case worker would continue until the state deemed no more visits were necessary. Buck and Esther had to walk a fine line because they didn't want to go through the nightmarish events that temporarily broke up their family. After the experience at the Chaney home, Katrina never again wanted to live with anybody other than her parents.

Chapter 21
Family Squabble

After Katrina returned home, it took a little time for everything to resume to normal. Esther was constantly in her husband's ear about the way he should deal with the children. She didn't want to go through the ordeal again. Buck also didn't want to hear it from his wife. He felt like the state had stripped him of any power to discipline his children. Though Buck completed the parenting classes, he learned very little as white people and black people have a huge cultural difference when it comes to disciplining their children. Buck didn't care whether or not the state was watching him; he would not tolerate his children to be disrespectful. However, learning a new way to discipline the kids was hard. Esther had to step in and play the role of disciplinarian. She also realized in order to have any leverage in the family she had to establish her own independence. Buck was always quick to throw the fact that he was the breadwinner for the family in her face and Esther was growing tired of it.

As a young girl, Esther was good at sewing and she could make a dress from scratch. Since Buck had a problem with her going out into the job market to get a job, she decided to have her business in her home. By then all her kids were in school and she was home most of the day, bored out of her mind after performing her daily chores around the house. Esther designed and sewed most of her dresses as well as her two daughters. The people at her church were always complimenting her on her designs and the special fabrics she would use to make her outfits. One day while talking to this woman, who was known as the queen of fashion and hats at the church, Esther was given the opportunity to make alterations to a dress the lady had purchased. She did such a great job, the lady decided to have Esther make all her dresses. She stopped buying clothes off the rack and Esther became her personal seamstress.

One thing led to another and word started getting out that Esther was a seamstress. The offers to make dresses for people at the church for a reasonable price started pouring in. Esther had established a clientele of over one hundred women in a short span of time. Her husband decided to buy her a "Singer" brand sewing machine as a Christmas gift one year. It was the best gift that Buck had ever given to his wife. The electric machine replaced the old manual sewing machine that Esther had purchased from a used dealer in the neighborhood. Her business would flourish beyond expectations.

Esther was gaining her independence and Buck didn't have to worry about working two jobs anymore. As things started looking up for Esther, she was slowly surpassing her husband's income. It was time for the family to have an extra car. Esther suggested that Buck get his learner's permit, which led to an argument because Buck didn't want his wife to know that he couldn't read well. Buck managed to get his learner's permit by paying someone to take the written exam for him without telling his wife. The white folks in Boston couldn't tell the difference between a light skinned black person and a dark skinned one. When the guy showed up to take the exam, they simply asked for an identification, which had no picture. However, Buck had to learn how to drive because he would be the one on the road driving his family around. It was hard for Buck to balance dishonesty with being a good Christian. It was a matter of convenience to him at that point.

Esther wanted so much to teach her husband how to drive, but his stubbornness got in the way. Buck was also not mechanically inclined, so he took out his frustration on his wife. After a few outbursts, Esther had enough. She suggested he pay an auto school in order to learn how to drive. The auto school instructor had never seen anyone as awkward as Buck behind the wheel. Buck would end up paying twice the amount of money most people paid to learn how to drive, because he required extra lessons. Getting his license was another hurdle. The first time he went, he couldn't parallel park the car, so the cop failed him. The second time he tried, he forgot to use his signal before making a right turn, he failed that time as well. By the third time, the cop had just grown frustrated with him and decided to give him the license anyway even though he had failed again.

After getting his license, Buck couldn't rely on Esther to run all the errands anymore. Besides, she had a prosperous business to run. He started to get a feel of how difficult life had been for his wife while he was at work trying to bring home "the bacon." Though he finally got a chance to experience it, he still showed no sympathy towards his wife. Esther was careful not to ever throw the fact that she was earning more money than Buck in his face. He was a proud man and she wanted him to feel like he was the king of his domain. Meanwhile, she started saving as much money as she could to help him pay his brother back for the loan he had given to purchase the house. Things were looking up for the Johnson family and Esther couldn't be happier.

However, the happiness would be short lived as Buck started to allow the fact that he was not certain about Katrina's paternity bother him. He started treating her differently and he would often make stupid comments to his wife about Katrina not resembling him in any way. Most of the time, he was making a mountain out of a molehill. Esther one day got so upset she told her husband, "If you really hate our child this much, why don't you go to the doctor and find out if she's yours? I'm tired of your crap. If you don't want to raise her, then leave." Buck was fuming inside because his wife had never talked to him like that. He never openly talked about the issue if front of Katrina, but she used to hear the whispers. She knew her daddy didn't love her like he loved the other children.

Esther had to show more affection towards Katrina than she did Eddy and Karen because she felt like Buck was distant from her. She really didn't know how to deal with the issue, but she tried her best to make her child feel loved and wanted. She often turned to prayer hoping that things between her and Buck would improve, but to no avail. Buck had his ways and there was no changing them. Esther even thought about leaving Buck. She had managed to save a couple of thousand dollars and she wanted badly to use that money to start a new life with her children. She could not. She thought about life without a husband, the children growing up without a father and how the church would look down on her, so she decided to stay with her husband.

Esther was also getting smarter. She realized that she needed to create a nest egg for herself in case Buck ever went way over the line with her. While she offered to give fifteen hundred dollars to go towards the payment to his brother, she kept five hundred dollars for herself in a secret hiding place in the house in case of an emergency. Esther was no longer that gullible chick that Buck had married. She was coming into her own and she matured into womanhood, leaving him behind in his little boy's world. Buck used the Bible and the word of God to instill fear in his wife and to keep her in the marriage. The guilt of breaking the marriage vows was like a cloud hanging over Esther's head.

The children clearly noticed the tension between their parents. Eddy would often try to comfort his mom with a hug throughout the day whenever she felt sad. The couple hadn't any clue how to deal with their issues. Buck was able to contain his temper to a certain degree when things got heated, but he had started to become verbally abusive and condescending towards his wife. He would call her stupid and dumb for no reason at all whenever something went wrong. It seemed as if his own insecurities were getting the best of him and he took it out on his family. Esther was fast becoming an extrovert and popular person in the church because of her talent, but Buck didn't know how to deal with that. He was just a plumber and very few people thought he deserved more respect than his wife. Though she wasn't a fashion icon, Esther's work was very much appreciated. She also started to improve her taste and style as well while Buck remained stuck in his own world.

Esther wanted to see the world and start experimenting different things. She no longer saw herself as the little victim that she once was. Buck was trying to stunt her growth and development, bur she wouldn't allow it. Esther knew the world consisted of more than the city of Boston and she wanted to see and expose her children to more.

It had been a while since Buck went to New York to see his family. Esther wanted so much to thank his brother in person for providing them with the money to buy the house, but she also wanted to see New York. She had heard about all the beautiful sites and the shows on Broadway. She wanted to experience it. She was finally able to convince Buck to take a trip with the family to New York. Buck saw it as a missed opportunity to earn more money over the weekend on some plumbing gigs. He hadn't taken time off from work in years. There was no reason for Buck to continue to work as hard as he once did because his wife was earning decent money. After Buck got his license, the family had purchased a better car, which he gave to his wife while he drove the older model. They decided that they would drive the newer car to New York. However, Buck was petrified of the idea of driving in New York. Esther showed no fear and he couldn't cower in front of his wife and children.

The four hour voyage didn't go so smoothly. Buck was still thinking about the two jobs he left undone and the possibility that his clients might hire another plumber in his absence. "You know I can be earning some extra money if I didn't have to come on this trip," he announced to his wife in the car while driving through Rhode Island. "Honey, you have not taken any time off in the past few years to do anything special with the children. We have never taken a vacation. Why don't you just enjoy the time off with your family?" she told him. "I still got to feed this family when I get back. Ain't nobody gonna put food on the table if I don't work. We ain't gonna be doing this all the time," he told his wife. The three children were in the back playing, but they could hear their father trying to stir things up with his wife. Esther wanted to put him in his place so badly because she knew that she had been contributing to the household, but she kept quiet because she wanted the kids to have a good time.

The complaining and pettiness from Buck would continue during the entire drive to New York. Esther tried her best to ignore him while focusing on the road. When they finally made it to Rochester to his brother's house, things would get worse. Esther had never been around Buck's family, so she didn't know what to expect. Unfortunately, when they got there everyone's spirit was down. BJ had fallen victim to the HIV virus and his mother was scared about losing her son. Back then, people thought of HIV as a plague and even family members kept their distance from the victims. Most of Buck's brothers and sisters had vacated the house fearing that they would somehow contract the disease. The only person who lived in the big house with his brother and mother was his younger sister.

At first, Mrs. Johnson didn't want to tell her son about BJ's illness, fearing that he might isolate his brother as well. Esther knew right away something was wrong because of the somber look on Mrs. Johnson's face. Diana,

Buck's youngest sister, was also teary eyed and looked sad.

There was a feeling of loneliness in the house. Buck's

siblings had forgotten about all that BJ had done to help

them. They forgot that he was the one who took them out of

the country and brought them up North for a better life and

opportunity. He had helped every single one of his brothers

and sisters and when he was on his death bed, they all

turned their backs on him.

Mrs. Johnson knew that Buck's reaction wouldn't be

any different. She cautioned her daughter not say anything

about BJ's condition. After getting over the excitement of

seeing his mother and sister, Buck was led to his brother's

room where he was resting. Unaware of his brother's

ailment, Buck gave his brother a hug and told him, "You're

gonna be all right, bro. You always know how to make

things better." He had no idea that his brother was living

with a death sentence. BJ knew that his mother hadn't told

Buck about his terminal illness. BJ was also angry that his

other siblings had left the house after they learned of his

HIV status. Since he knew he was dying, he didn't care

about anybody's opinion anymore. If they weren't to show

any gratitude towards him, it was their business. "Did my

mother explain to you that I'm gonna die?" he said to Buck.

Esther and Mrs. Johnson decided to walk out of the room with her children because it was a too grown conversation for them. It also seemed like a personal matter that should be discussed between the two brothers only. "What do you mean you're gonna die? You're BJ. You always know how to survive. You know how to make everything ok, you're not gonna die," Buck said like a little brother hoping that his big brother had the solution.

BJ had been angry with his family since the deterioration of his health. If it wasn't for his mother, he probably would die alone. BJ had become frail and had lost almost thirty percent of his weight. He was one of the first few victims who had contracted HIV through homosexual contact. His partner and lover had also died of AIDS. No one ever suspected that BJ was gay, not even his mother. He never brought his business to Rochester with him because he knew his brothers were prejudice against gays and they would hate him for it. BJ kept an apartment in Greenwich Village in the city and that was the place where he spent most of his time with his lover. He never outted himself to the world. He wanted to keep his private affairs private.

BJ was not the typical homosexual other than the fact that he was always well-dressed and wore the latest fashion designs available on the market. After his mentor died, Junior led a wild life. As part of his therapy, he started partying heavily and was secretly well-known in the gay community as a party animal. He took part in wild gay orgies, and did things that were risky to his health. HIV and AIDS hadn't yet come to the forefront of national news. Few people in the gay community were aware of the deadly disease. It wasn't until it was too late that many homosexuals in New York and San Francisco started to realize the severity of the disease. By then, many people had fallen victim and the government was putting the blame for the disease squarely on the gay community's shoulder. Most of them resented that fact, but nothing was being done to slow down the disease. People were scared, but many of them didn't think it could happen to them. It wasn't until Rock Hudson died that the gay community started to grasp the seriousness of the disease.

The death of Rock Hudson forced Hollywood and the mainstream media to pay more attention, but it also added fuel to the fire. A closeted homosexual for most of his career, Rock Hudson continued to portray the leading man role in Hollywood until his death. It would have been career suicide if it was known that he was gay. There would be many more Hollywood stars to die from AIDS. Junior was no different from the likes of Rock Hudson. He would bring his female friends home to his family and acted like he was a ladies' man in New York City. Blessed with a great sense of style, good looks, great height and perfect articulation, he was almost the epitome of a Hollywood star. BJ would bring a new woman home every other month to his family. They were gorgeous women who worked as models, actresses and in the arts. His brothers were so envious of him. However, most of these women shared a platonic relationship with BJ. He was not interested in them. He brought them home for show and tell in order to fool his family. His mother often wondered why he didn't settle down with one of these gorgeous women, and why he didn't have any kids. BJ would always use work to justify his not being able to settle down and get married. He was a workaholic who was very successful at what he did. BJ took great care of his entire family. Any of them with a dream was encouraged to pursue that dream. He helped finance the education for those who wanted to go to school. And for the ones who got married and settled down, he helped pay for their homes. There was no limit as to what he would do to help his family.

While many homosexual/bisexual men today choose to be on the down low, BJ never wanted to fool a woman into thinking that he was into her. He was real with himself and knew that he only liked men. Because of acceptance, he was forced to lie to his family and his worse nightmare came true when it was found out that he had contracted AIDS. BJ had never mentioned to his family that he was gay, but they automatically made the connection because the media had dubbed AIDS a gay disease. His siblings wouldn't come near him because they thought he would infect them. They even warned their mother that she would catch the disease as well if she continued to care for her dying son. BJ found out the hard way that all great deeds always go unrewarded.

As angry as BJ had become, he didn't give a damn about how Buck would feel about him. As he lay on his bed watching his brother, he was bracing himself for a reaction he knew would be all too familiar. Buck loved his brother and he appreciated everything that he had done for him, but he was still an ignorant soul like the rest of his siblings who had turned their backs on the brother who helped changed their livelihood and status in life. "I'm a gay man and I'm HIV positive, Buck," BJ blurted out to his brother, hoping to get the discomfort over and done with. "What! You're a faggot?" Buck screamed out, without realizing he had just insulted his brother. "Exactly, bro. You can do like the rest of them and just walk out and never return," he said to

Buck. He would prove him right. Buck didn't even bother unloading the car. He ushered his family back in the car and said goodbye to his mother before heading back to Boston. The visit to New York was short and quick.

Mrs. Johnson divulged to Esther that her son was HIV positive and the emotional roller coaster that she had been riding since her son fell ill. Though Esther was a little more understanding than Buck, she didn't try to convince him to stay because she didn't want her children in the house. She feared that they might catch the disease even if they drink from the same drinking glass as BJ. As far as she was concerned, everything in that house was contaminated. She felt sorry for BJ, but she didn't want to stick around to find out whether or not she could be exposed to the disease. The media had very little information about the disease and everyone was scared. Buck couldn't wait to get home to wash because he had hugged his brother. He felt like he was walking around with AIDS on his body. He couldn't wash his hands enough before he left Rochester.

Chapter 22
Humiliation

As Buck and his wife hurried out of the house to get back on the road to Boston, the children seemed baffled. They were baffled by the idea that they had sat in the car for a little over four hours only to have a forty-five minute visit with their grandmother. "Mommy, why did we have to leave grandma's house so soon?" Eddy asked while the couple headed back home. "No reason, sweetie. Mommy and Daddy have to get back home," Esther lied. Katrina was a little too bright and too old to believe that BS. "We left 'cause daddy was mad at uncle BJ because he was sick. Daddy, why did you get mad at Uncle BJ because he was sick?" Katrina asked. Buck wasn't the type to have any type of conversation with his kids. He talked and they had to listen and that was that. Buck didn't know what to say to his daughter, so he kept quiet, but Katrina wouldn't let up. "Look, you ask too many dag on questions. Just hush up," Buck told his daughter in a not-so-friendly tone. Katrina knew that she had better not ask any more questions. Esther shot her husband a look as if to say, "Don't you dare talk to my child like that." The kids would not get an explanation from their parents about the brief visit with their grandmother and uncle. Buck pulled into a rest stop to make sure that the kids were fed at McDonald's.

All curiosity about the trip was removed as the kids dug into their Happy Meals. While Buck tried to unwrap one of the sandwiches for Karen, he almost inadvertently swerved out of his lane on I-95 North off the road. Unfortunately, it was a mistake that would bring about humiliation in front of his children. A state trooper stationed about one hundred yards ahead noticed the swerving of the car and immediately merged into traffic in pursuit of Buck's car. It took Buck but five seconds to notice the flashing lights behind him as the police officer got closer. His wife advised him to pull over to the side of the road to deal with the traffic stop. "Sir, can I see your license and registration please?" asked the officer. Buck who had never been in serious trouble with the law, was nervous as heck as he reached for his license and registration. "Sir, please open your glove compartment slowly and keep your hands where I can see them," ordered the white officer. It was obvious that Buck was a family man, but the officer wanted to make sure that Buck understood he was not his equal as a man. "What seems to be the problem, officer," Esther asked. "I will ask the questions. You just sit tight with your mouth shut while I do my job," the officer replied with an attitude.

The officer had crossed the line and Buck was not going to allow him to disrespect his wife. "I don't appreciate the way you're talking to my wife," Buck told him. "Sir, step out of the car," the officer ordered. "Step outta the car, for what?" Buck asked. As Buck took his time to get out of the car as urged by his wife to keep the peace, the officer started pulling him by this collar out of the car. Buck never physically reacted, but he knew that the officer didn't really stand a chance against him. "You people always want to disobey orders. I'm gonna teach you," the officer says. He also placed a call for backup. Fortunately for Buck, the responding officer was another black officer who came and took control of the situation. At the pleading of Mrs. Johnson, the officer was able to let Buck go with just a warning. This was one of the few times that a black officer had stood up for what's right and Buck was lucky. Buck was lucky that he had his wife and kids in the car with him. The black officer who was also a family man had been subjected to the same maltreatment weeks earlier as he drove to Boston from his home state in Connecticut. He was wearing civilian clothing when he was pulled over in Rhode Island near Providence. A racist cop didn't even care that he was a fellow officer as he berated him for speeding in front of his family. That experience shaped the mind and view of that officer forever. He knew that he couldn't allow another black man to be subjected to that travesty of injustice as long as he could help it. However, the humiliation Buck suffered in front of his children couldn't be erased from their young minds.

The rest of the ride back to Boston was very quiet as the family tried to cope with the nightmare that took place with the police officer. Buck was angry and felt like he couldn't escape racism no matter what part of the country he was in. White people had shaped his entire life and they continued to do so even when he was out driving with his family. Buck needed an outlet to let out his frustration, but he had none. He kept everything bottled in and tried to cope as best as he could with the different situations. Any other man would've exploded under those circumstances.

Chapter 23
Family Life

The Johnson family returned to Boston to a life that now seemed more normal than ever. Their neighbors were still angry that they had moved into the neighborhood, but there was nothing they could do about it. Buck was now dealing with the possible death of his brother and wrestled with the idea of attending his brother's funeral. Esther thought he should at least pay his last respects. Buck contemplated how he would deal with the situation. Meanwhile, the three children were getting older and the parents were trying to figure out their individual personalities. Eddy was the quiet boy who did everything his parents asked of him. His dad was very proud when he was born, as any father would, because the family name would be carried for one more generation. However, Buck would not be the model dad that Eddy needed. As a young boy, Eddy spent most of his time with his mother. His dad was always too tired to play with him or he would choose to watch basketball over him. Eddy had no choice but to become a sports fanatic in order to spend time with his dad.

Eddy was on his way to becoming an introvert. He spent the rest of his time playing with his sister, Karen, who took care of him like he was her child. Karen and Eddy attended the same elementary school and she would often beat up the boys who tried to bully her older brother. Eddy was more passive-aggressive. It took a lot to provoke him, and when he was pushed to his limit, he was out of control. Far from a troublemaker, Eddy never wanted to upset his parents. At school, he had also become the teacher's pet and many of the other children resented him for it. He was a people pleaser and forever the smart Alec when he needed to be. His wit was endless and his bright smile melted his teacher's heart.

Eddy was the most honest of the three Johnson children. He would tell his mother and father the truth almost one hundred percent of the time, even when he was dead wrong. The only time that Eddy was forced to lie was when his sisters forced him into a pact to save their own asses. Often times, though, his parents could see that he had been talked into it. The boy just couldn't lie with a straight face.

Karen was the toughest of the three children. She had a temper and she was quick to act out. She was also Ms. Attitude. Karen just knew that she was special and felt like she was the most beautiful princess. She would stand in front of the mirror and dance all day. Sometimes she would turn her room upside down by playing dress-up in front of the mirror in her room. Her family was often amused by her actions. Karen also had a smart mouth and was a little hard-headed.

At school, the teachers often had to ask her to bring a parent with her because she was always crossing the line with them. Karen defied most rules and she relished in the fact that she was labeled a rebel. A rebel she had also become. She had run-ins with most of the girls at her school and some of the boys too. She didn't back down from anybody and she had a mouth that could scare a whole crew away. Karen always took things too far with everyone. She once flipped the bird to a teacher because the teacher told her to keep quiet. Another time, she slapped this girl silly because the girl said something about her clothes. Karen didn't mess around.

If there was ever a daddy's little girl, Karen would be it. However, Buck left no room for Karen to become daddy's little girl. The lack of affection and the emotional distance between him and his kids created a wedge. Buck just wasn't an emotional person and Karen would often call him on it. "Daddy, how come you don't tell mommy you love her?" she once asked her father. Buck didn't really know what to say, so he ignored the question. Then Karen came back with another question, "Do you love me, daddy?" "Of course, I love you," Buck answered. "Do you love mommy?" she asked again. "I do love mommy," Buck answered. "Do you love Eddy?" Karen continued. "I love Eddy too,' Buck told her. "What about Katrina, do you love Katrina, daddy?" she asked with curiosity. Karen could sense the discomfort from Buck when she asked the question. Katrina who was standing a few feet away in the same room could feel it even more. Buck paused for a few seconds before saying, "I love all of you." He didn't exactly answer Karen's question, but he gave her an answer.

Katrina had always felt like the black sheep of the family. She was the brightest and most promising of all the children. Katrina was actually intellectually gifted. She had never been below the top one percentile of her class since she started school. Making the honor roll was the norm for Katrina. Most of her teachers labeled her studious, bright, intelligent or smart. Katrina lived up to the names by keeping a perfect A average from the time she started grade school. Her parents never had to worry about any problems at school because she was a model student.

A shy and naturally quiet girl with the demeanor of an innocent angel, Katrina couldn't hurt a fly. However, there was always one thing eating away at her heart. Katrina could sense that her father didn't love her like he loved her siblings. Often times, she felt like Cinderella without the fairytale. As the oldest child, she was responsible for many of the chores around the house as her mother's business grew. By the time she was ten years old, she was checking her brother and sister's homework, making sure they were fed, mopping the floor, doing the dishes, ironing clothes and cleaning up after her dad and siblings. Her mother thought she was teaching her daughter to be responsible and how to be domesticated so she could find a good husband, but Katrina resented her for that. She felt she was being used while her younger siblings had fun. Her dad was even tougher on her as he required Katrina to pick up after him as well as herself. He once promised to beat her silly if she didn't clean up a mess he made. Even his tone was different when he addressed Katrina. The authority in his voice was pervasive as he tried to instill fear in his daughter. Katrina was no dummy; she noticed the difference in treatment right away.

She kept to herself and didn't want to be bothered. She did as she was told, but the resentment did not go away. By the time Katrina started middle school, she was developing as a young woman and the boys in her sixth grade class started to notice her. Katrina was a pretty girl and she was very shapely for her age. The boys didn't really know how to talk to her, so they teased her instead. She was very conservative in her looks as her parents did not allow her to wear pants or jeans to school. She either wore dresses or skirts to school. Still, her natural beauty couldn't be denied. Katrina was also teased often by her peers because she was so bright. Being labeled a nerd didn't bother her as much as her father didn't appreciate her intelligence. He would call her stupid whenever she did something wrong and he had a lot of animosity towards her because of the past involvement with the Department of Social Services.

For the most part, Katrina kept to herself and buried herself in her books. She had also developed a voracious appetite for reading. She was reading one book every single week. As her mind and vocabulary expanded, Katrina felt no longer challenged at her school. She wanted to attend a better school. She went to her parents and told them that she would like to take the entrance exam for Latin Academy. Her parents had heard about Latin Academy being a good school, but they weren't sure how good the school was. Going from the Lewenberg Middle school to Latin Academy would be a big change for Katrina. Not only was there going to be more academic challenges, there was also going to be a change in her travels. Latin Academy was located miles from her school and she would have to catch the school bus every morning to get there. Katrina had never ridden the bus to school by herself and that would present a serious challenge for her.

It was agreed upon by her parents that Katrina could attend Latin Academy if she did well enough on the entrance exam. Katrina studied and prepared for the exam just like she normally did for any other exam. After taking the exam, it took a few weeks for her to get the results. Of course, she had performed as expected. She scored well enough to be accepted into Latin Academy. Katrina was excited about her new school. Her mother was very proud of her. Buck was happy as well, but he wasn't as emotional as Esther about the whole thing. Katrina couldn't wait for the school year to be over so she could attend her new school. Life as she knew it was about to change for her. There would be new challenges and she wouldn't be the shining star in her class anymore.

All that Katrina was used to was out the window. She had to start anew and the adjustment was difficult at first, to say the least. Her classes suddenly weren't so easy and she struggled with her work. In the past, Katrina never needed help with her homework because she paid close enough attention during class and she was able to absorb the lessons very easily from her teachers. However, at Latin Academy the students were a little more advanced and the teachers assumed everyone in their classes were on par with each other. It was a difficult moment for Katrina because she couldn't go home and get help from her parents either. Neither of her parents had made it far in school and they couldn't even comprehend the adjustment that Katrina had to make from being the smartest in the class to becoming a lame duck. For the first time in her life, Katrina had to learn that her parents had not gone far in school even though they had been preaching to their kids the importance of an education.

Esther didn't struggle as much as Buck to let her kids know that she didn't get far in school. She wanted to use her lack of an education as motivation for her kids to achieve more. She told them about her struggles in life and how she had to become a seamstress in order to earn a living. She wasn't complaining about her profession, but she wanted her children to know that there was more to life than what they saw at home. Buck had never told his wife how far he had gotten in school and he wasn't about to reveal that little bit of truth to her just because Katrina was having difficulties in school. Buck was already uncomfortable with the fact that his wife was earning more money than him from a home-based business. He damn sure wasn't going to tell her that he wasn't more educated than her. Still, Katrina had a problem and she needed to find a way to solve it. Her mom suggested she asked for extra help at school or even get a tutor if she needed one.

Katrina took her mom's advice and started hanging out with this other kid who lived on her block and also attended the same school. The kid was very bright and he was the one responsible for helping Katrina catch up in school. Once she caught up, she was back to her old self again and she became a star in school in very little time. The teachers took notice quickly of her intelligence and she was fast becoming the teachers' favorite student again. Meanwhile, her new buddy, who looked so much like a nerd because of his Coke bottle glasses, was starting to become attracted to Katrina. His name was Henry.

Chapter 24
Henry

Katrina never even took notice of Henry in her class. He wasn't the standout athletic type that the ladies gushed over. He wasn't even cute, according to the girls at the school. Henry was simply studious and plain. His parents didn't have much money, so they bought him the best brand of clothes that their money could afford from Zaire's, a store chain similar to K-Mart. Zaire's was the affordable store for low income families. However, their clothes were the butt of all jokes to all the kids in the Boston area. While Henry didn't put too much emphasis on the brand of clothes he wore, the rest of the students at his school did. Most of his peers, who weren't much better off than him financially, would tease him and laugh at him for wearing Matt Andrews sneakers and corduroy pants to school. Henry had grown accustom to it and became immune to the teasing. He was a very dark skinned boy with peasy hair, braces and an awkward demeanor. Henry just wasn't too comfortable around people.

Katrina saw Henry for the first time after about a week since she had been traveling to school. They rode the same school bus everyday, but she never paid any attention to him. They even boarded the bus at the same stop. One day while walking the block to her house, another boy started teasing Henry. Katrina quickly took notice and told the guy to leave Henry alone. From that point on, she started sitting next to Henry on the bus and they became friends. Katrina also learned that she shared most of her classes with Henry and he was an honor roll student. She decided to tell him about her difficulties at school and he offered to help her. Katrina was also surprised to learn that another African American family had moved to her street and she was happy about that. She couldn't wait to get home to tell her parents. She felt that her dad was always battling these white folks by himself and now he possibly had help.

Katrina and Henry also had more in common than they even knew. While Henry's family didn't focus too much on the latest brand of clothes for their son, they made sure he was clean everyday. Katrina's situation was not much different. Until her mother started sewing her skirts, dresses and blouses, they were buying clothes for her from Woolworth, which was a basic equal of Zaire's. Katrina had gotten teased in the past for wearing less expensive clothes, so she understood what Henry was going through. The biggest difference between them was the fact that Katrina was a pretty girl and Henry wasn't such an attractive boy, at first. As time went by, Katrina and Henry became closer. She started to see beyond his looks and she appreciated Henry, the human being.

Henry had never had a friend before and he treasured the friendship he shared with Katrina. Like all boys going through the pubescent years, Henry started to develop a crush on Katrina. Over time, he started having a hard time looking her straight in the eyes. His bashfulness was cute to her and from that a teenaged love developed. Katrina and Henry looked like two awkward kids who were just happy to be around each other. Henry would bring candy for Katrina in the morning and they would sit together on the bus holding hands. The "Now and Later" candy brand was especially popular among low income families back in the day and Henry would buy enough candy to last Katrina through the day. Their relationship never went farther than holding hands for the first year and a half. They couldn't talk much on the phone because Buck wouldn't allow Katrina to talk to boys on the phone. However, Katrina found a way to see Henry when she told her father that he was the one who helped her get adjusted at her new school, and with her homework.

Buck and Esther never thought that anything beyond a friendship would develop between Katrina and Henry because they looked so awkward together. As any parents would wish, Esther thought her daughter would want to be with a more attractive boy. Katrina, at that point, had already gone beneath the surface and she really liked Henry. She didn't care that the whole world didn't think Henry was attractive. He was her special friend and she enjoyed spending time with him.

Chapter 25
Amazing Grace

God had finally called BJ to heaven and the suffering and humiliation had finally come to an end. BJ no longer had to deal with the prejudices of his own family and the strangers who looked down on him without knowing a thing about him. Even the pastor of the church where BJ was a member for many years almost refused to perform the service at his funeral. BJ was a condemned man and even in death he was being judged. When the word was leaked that BJ was a gay man, most of the people at his church wanted nothing to do with his funeral. He was the same man who had no problem signing a check for thousands of dollars when the church needed money for repairs. He was the same man who provided funding for their youth ministry as well as other events at the church. He was shunned because of his personal choice and way of life.

While so many people didn't want to be around BJ when he was sick, even more were curious about his wealth because he died a very rich man. BJ had helped his entire family, but when he needed them most, they were afraid of him and they left him to die alone. Every single one of them benefited from his kindness and generosity. BJ held nothing back when it came to his family. He would do anything to help them. One of his brothers once called him a "faggot," and BJ simply said, "I forgive you because you don't know how to love. It was never taught to us." BJ lived a secret life until his illness and he regretted keeping that secret for so long. He died proudly and happily because he felt that a burden had been lifted off his shoulders when he finally came out of the closet. Mrs. Johnson was the epitome of unconditional love. She cared for her son with very little concern for her own health. BJ often had to force her to wear gloves to keep from getting exposed to the disease. She never believed that her son could infect her in any way.

The whispers about BJ's net worth were getting louder as the day of his funeral approached. All those siblings who turned their backs on him were now trying to find out what was in BJ's will for them. When he died, everyone in the family owed him money. He was not the type to press someone about a debt owed, especially family members. Many of them knew that their debt ended with his death, but they wanted more. Buck and Esther still owed over ten thousand dollars to BJ when he died. In BJ's will, he wrote that he would forgo all those debts if his family came together for one day for his wake and funeral. He was a smart man who had drawn up contracts for every single member of his family that he had ever loaned money to. The stipulation in his will asked that all money be paid to his estate if a family member failed to attend his funeral. Of course, Mrs. Johnson had to relay the testament in the will to her children.

BJ had planned and paid for this elaborate will and funeral, and all his gay friends were invited to celebrate his life. He gave his mother a list of names of people he wanted at his funeral and he asked her to honor his last request. Some of the most flaming, homosexual friends of BJ were invited to his funeral and his brothers and sisters would have no choice but to entertain his friends. They had to be nice to them. BJ even had a stipulation for his church. The church would be granted $100,000.00 if they welcomed everyone to the church for the funeral. BJ wanted to leave behind a legacy of bringing folks together regardless of race, creed, religion or sexual orientation. His list included names of prominent politicians, musicians, singers, actors, writers and other notables in society. Being the apprentice to one of the most famous playwrights in New York City had its perks and BJ networked his way to their pockets.

He left money to every organization that he could help, but most of all, he wanted to leave money to a special organization that helped teenagers deal with their sexuality. The suicide rate among gay teenagers was alarming at the time and BJ was always a major figure helping to alleviate their pain with monetary as well as physical assistance. Whenever and wherever he was needed, he made it a point to be there. Most of the fifty-million dollar net worth he left behind went to many different nonprofit organizations. Mrs. Johnson was also set up with a trust fund that would pay her a comfortable allowance for the rest of her life. BJ's siblings were very disappointed that he left them nothing, but they still had to attend his funeral. BJ also left one of his play directors in charge of his company until the grandchildren in the family were old enough to inherit the company. Buck's children and his sisters' children in Virginia were the only new generation in the family and BJ wanted to continue the legacy of wealth as well as business ownership. However, no one would find out about that part of the will until the oldest grandchild, would turn twenty five. The firm responsible for BJ's estate would have to make every effort to locate the oldest grandchild first. Katrina was way down the line because the twin girls had given birth to their kids a year into their marriage.

As planned, BJ's wake and funeral was festive. Some of his most colorful friends showed up to celebrate his life. There were flamboyant as well as closeted homosexuals among the crowd. All of BJ's siblings came, including Buck and his family. Buck more or less came because he didn't want to pay the loan back to BJ's estate. That little stipulation in the will forced everybody's hands, even the pastor at the church who couldn't wait to get his hands on the $100,000.00 endowment. There were cries coming from everywhere. Many people cared about BJ. Even though he died with very few people around him, he had many friends. The horse and carriage that carried his casket was followed by a line of cars long enough to shut down the whole city of Rochester, New York. His mother couldn't be more proud of her son.

Ignorance had been the root of the very existence of the Johnson family for many years. It wasn't until BJ's death that the family started to realize the darkness that they had been living in for so long. The Johnson family had never seen an array of people from so many different backgrounds. BJ had brought together a melting pot in death that any politician would dream of. He finally was a celebrated man who gave more to his family in death than he did when he was alive. Whether or not BJ's family took the lesson or opportunity that he exposed them to and applied them to their lives, would be up to them. He did everything that he could. Though he didn't line everyone's pocket with dead presidents as they expected, BJ tried to teach them a valuable lesson in tolerance.

All of BJ's siblings worried about their mother and the agony that she went through before BJ passed away. But Mrs. Johnson was her happiest when she stood next to her son's coffin. She could see peace on his face and for that she just smiled instead of shedding tears. She knew that her son was on his way to heaven and she couldn't wait to join him a few years later.

Chapter 26
Back To Life

The funeral was over. Buck and his family spent a couple more days with his mother before leaving for Boston. The funeral gave Buck and his children a chance to connect with his brothers and sisters that he hadn't seen in a long time. Buck was never the type of man to reach out to his siblings. After he got married, his focus was his family and that was it. Occasionally, he would pick up the phone to call his mother to check up on her, but most of the time it was at his wife's urging. Esther had also developed a close relationship with Mrs. Johnson. Whenever the two of them got together they would spend most of their time in Mrs. Johnson's garden, located in the backyard of the house. Mrs. Johnson was very fond of Esther and she would often tell Esther to be patient with Buck because he came from a rough upbringing. Buck didn't tell his wife much about the murder of his daddy by one of his brothers or the brutal treatment he received at the hands of his father. Like most men, he tried to tough it out and acted like he wasn't affected at all.

Mrs. Johnson was a wise woman and she understood the toll that the physical abuse took on her children at the hands of her husband. Though not formally educated, she also understood the psychological ramifications of her own mistreatment at the hands of her husband. Like most black folks anywhere in the world, Mrs. Johnson turned to prayer to help deal with her issues. She would often pray to God and ask The Lord to watch over her children. Every action or inaction was justified in the eyes of God. Mrs. Johnson would often contradict herself when she prayed. In one instance when she found out that BJ was dying of AIDS, she thought the Lord would provide a cure. And when He didn't provide a cure, Mrs. Johnson resonated with the fact that it was time for The Lord to call her son home. Black folks always justified The Lord's action one way or another. Mrs. Johnson even wondered why so many Africans around the world live in the worst conditions possible, while white folks seem to live in the life of luxury compared to the substandard conditions that Black folks are living in. She would often say, "Lord, you would never give us problems that you know we can't handle. I guess you're just telling us how strong we really are by making us face all these problems." That was her way of justifying the struggle of all black people around the world; the HIV crisis in Africa, the

- 157 -

tribal wars, famine, the health crisis and every other reason that black people die around the world daily.

Mrs. Johnson believed in her prayers. She would tell Esther that everything was possible through prayer and the Lord would always find a way to provide. She also raised her son that way. Esther had been raised that way by her parents as well. The Lord and the church had always played a significant role in her life. She had planned on raising her children the same way, to believe in the word of God and the church. The church was most important to the Johnson family. That tradition would continue for many more generations to come.

While Esther was spending time with her mother-in-law, Buck was reconnecting with his brothers and sisters. It had been so long since they spent time together, every one of them seemed like strangers to each other. The two youngest ones were now grown adults and the sisters from Virginia had adult children. It seemed as if time had passed them by. The family seemed disoriented because they never dealt with the issues that affected their lives while growing up.

Every member of the Johnson family seemed to have been dealing with some personal demons. Gerald had never gotten over the fact that he had killed his father. BJ spent a lot of money for Gerald's defense. The newly hired attorney was able to get Gerald off on a technicality of insanity after he served a couple of years in prison. After he was released from prison, Gerald moved to Rochester with the rest of his family. Life for Gerald would never be the same. He started working with BJ's production company, but he soon became a slacker. He couldn't focus and he often had to relive the situation where he shot his dad. He found refuge in a whisky bottle that he couldn't seem to put down. His life withered right before his eyes as he tried to cope with life and the reality of what he had done. The other siblings were no better off, but everyone managed to keep their problems private, except for Gerald who was hugging a bottle of whisky the whole time he was at the house in Rochester. A couple of siblings wanted to say something to him about his drinking, but for fear of being a victim, they left it alone. Gerald had become very boisterous and confrontational due to his drinking and no one wanted to deal with him.

While the family tried as much as they could to get along, the squabbles were inevitable and arguments broke out amongst them. At the end of the day, they all realized they were better off away from each other, even though they loved each other. Mrs. Johnson tried as much as she could to keep the peace, but her children were grown. She could no longer control them. She tried to appeal to their sensitive sides, but too many of them were insensitive for her to get through. It was a total debacle and she felt embarrassed in front of the spouses.

Gerald had squandered all the money he received from BJ and was on the brink of homelessness. BJ had a particularly soft spot for Gerald when he was alive because he understood what it took for Gerald to finally end his dad's life. If BJ had enough courage, he would have been the one to take out his father. And for that reason, BJ continued to take care of Gerald until his death. Now that BJ was gone, Gerald was about to be the leech sucking the blood out of his mother. She worried about the well-being of her son and she secretly told him to come see her whenever he needed money. Poor Gerald lived in a rooming house with very few possessions, without a wife or children. His drinking never allowed him to establish a family or a career. There were times when BJ would see him standing on a street corner while driving through Rochester. He never left Rochester because he wouldn't survive anywhere else.

Mrs. Johnson knew that so much had gone wrong in her kids' lives, but she couldn't accept failure from them.

Gerald was the worst of all of them, but the others only learned to mask their issues. Most of them lived miserable lives and many of them were physically abusive to their wives. The women hid their pain and concealed their bruises from the other siblings. The cycle of abuse didn't stop and could not be stopped because none of them was willing to deal with the issues.

Mrs. Johnson would die almost five years after BJ passed. She was happy to see that most of her children had grown to live as adults. Her life was celebrated by all her children. She was always worried about Gerald. She only prayed that he could take care of himself after she'd pass on. The house that BJ had left for her in Rochester was given to Gerald, who later lost it because of his drinking.

Chapter 27
Back To Reality

After a couple of days in Rochester, reality started to set in for Buck. He started to realize that he was part of a dysfunctional family. He couldn't take it anymore. As much as he wanted to spend a few more days with his mother, he had to leave to get his peace of mind. Buck loaded up his car with his wife and children and headed to Boston. This time around, Buck made sure he gave the police no reason to mess with him. His eyes were fixated on the road and the speedometer. He never exceeded the speed limit and he followed every rule of the road until got home that night.

Unlike some of his brothers, Buck didn't expect to receive any money from his brother. He had no idea that his brother was so rich until he went to the funeral. Buck was content with not having to pay the remainder of the money he owed his brother. Without the cloud of a mortgage hanging over their heads, Esther now wanted to travel with her family and see the rest of the country, even the world, if time permitted. Other than New York, Esther had never been anywhere. Money was not a big issue anymore and she wanted to start splurging a little. The generic brand of cereal was no longer an option; generic brand for any food was no longer an option. Esther wanted a taste of the good life. Buck, however, worried more about a rainy day than anything. His tomorrow was not promised and he wasn't ready to start splurging. Be it as it may, Esther earned her own money and she wanted to do whatever she wanted with it. That attitude left too much room for contempt and arguments. She never wanted to defy her husband. Instead, she started secretly treating her children to a movie while her husband was at work. She would drive to Paragon Park in the summer so the kids could have some fun. Since Buck didn't talk much to his children, he never knew what they got into during the day.

Buck had formed the habit of watching sports when he got home from work until he went to sleep. He was a big fan of basketball, baseball and football. When there was no sport on TV, he would read his Bible. The family attended church three times a week for service, Bible studies, and other special events. Buck had become very religious and buried himself in the word of God. Though he couldn't read well, Buck had managed to study the whole Bible. Whether he was able to retain the information because of the church, no one ever knew for sure at that point.

While the church dominated the Johnson household, there was another reality that Buck had to deal with; the reality that his daughter was becoming a teenager. Katrina was growing up and growing up fast. The changes in her body were obvious that she was developing from a young girl to a woman, but Esther and her husband didn't give her the attention she deserved. While Esther's business was booming because of the church, she also became more involved in church activities. She would bring her children to every church event, hoping the exposure to the church and the word of God would rear her children, a common mistake that most religious families make. Esther and Buck negated their duties as parents because the word of God was supposed to be getting through to their children.

Eddy, the forever mama's boy, wouldn't do anything wrong. He was as straight laced as they come. Karen was the troublemaker of the family and she was labeled as such. Buck and his wife focused more on Karen than they did the other two children. At times, Katrina felt neglected by them because her issues were never discussed and her family expected her to be well-adjusted at school. With that came all the other problems. As Katrina started to develop the body of a woman, many of her peers started to take notice. More importantly, Henry and the other boys started to notice Katrina. The attention Katrina was receiving couldn't be denied and she enjoyed every minute of it. Katrina was on a path to discover and enjoy her womanhood. Her curves couldn't be denied and her beauty was very fresh and natural, for a young lady.

Chapter 28
Katrina And The Boys

Katrina did not start showing any defiance towards her parents until she started the eighth grade. It was then that she started to discover fashion and everything else associated with pop culture. Meanwhile, Henry was also developing as a young man. He was no longer interested in holding hands with Katrina. One day after begging her parents to allow her to go to the movies with Henry, Katrina got the surprise of her life. While she was sitting in the darkness of the movie theatre with Henry, she could feel his breath around her neck. Henry wanted to dive in for a kiss, but he didn't know how. He finally positioned his face next to hers so that his lips would land on hers if she turned to the left to look at him. It worked. Henry had gotten his first kiss from Katrina by accident and through careful planning. Katrina was almost shocked, but she wasn't mad. In fact, she had thought about the possibility of sharing a kiss with Henry. From the time she met him, he had grown from a scrawny, awkward looking boy to a decent looking fella. His teeth had come together nicely after he took off the braces. However, Henry was still wearing a retainer. He had also developed some grooming habits. He kept his hair cut very short and lined it every other week.

Henry, like Katrina, was also taking notice of the fashion trends. It was time to let go of the bobo sneakers, the plaid shirts and the corduroy pants in the summer time. Henry was mowing lawns, shoveling snow and doing anything else around the neighborhood he could, to earn extra money. By then, over half the neighbors on the street were black. The white folks slowly, but surely fled the street as a few black families started to move in. It was almost like the fleecing of Hyde Park. As Henry earned a little cash, he started to treat himself to some brand name clothing. The hottest brands at the time were Lee, Levis, Jordache, Calvin Klein, Sergio Valente, Polo, Izod, Le Tigre and a few others. Henry kept it real; he bought the lower brands like Lee and Levis. The rap group, Run DMC, made the Lee brand very famous and it was an affordable brand. Henry bought Lee jeans in every color and style. He also bought Polo, Izod and other brands of shirts to wear. His sneaker of choice was the famous shell toe Adidas, which were very popular in Boston back in the 80's. While doing all the splurging, Henry didn't forget about Katrina. He bought clothing items for Katrina as well, but he knew she couldn't wear them. She made him aware of her parents' rules regarding fashion.

There was no way Katrina wasn't going to wear the clothes that Henry was buying her. She felt like a hungry child standing in front of a plate of her favorite food, but couldn't take a bite. Forbidden to wear jeans or any other risqué looking clothing, Katrina was fighting a battle of will and disobedience. She needed to find a way to not only wear the clothes that Henry was buying for her, but also to keep them. She devised a plan to have the clothes stored in her locker at school. She would change in the morning when she got to school into the fashionable clothes that Henry bought her, and then change back to her boring clothes before heading home. The only problem with her plan was the fact that her clothes would eventually need washing. Where would she wash them and how? She wondered. She came up with yet another plan. For a while her mother had been forcing her to learn how to do the laundry and she hated it. This was her opportunity to finally enjoy something that she could also benefit from. Katrina volunteered to go to the Laundromat every Saturday with her mother for three weeks. On the fourth week, she decided to tell her mother something that she never saw coming. "Mommy, I'm fourteen years old now, I think I need more responsibilities," she told her mom. "What do you mean, what kind of responsibility are you talking about?" her mother asked. "I need to do something that I can feel proud of. Something on my own," she said. "Well, what is it that you think you can do on your own?" "Ok. Here's what I'm thinking…I know that you do the laundry every Saturday and then you have to come home and cook and work. How about you drop me off at the Laundromat and I can do the laundry every Saturday?" "Are you sure you're ready to take on that responsibility? I know how you hate doing the laundry," her mom told her. "I know, but you need the help and I need to start helping more with the household chores," she told her mom.   Her little conniving plan worked perfectly. However, her mom would allow her to go to the Laundromat only if her younger sister, Karen, could go with her.

Katrina never anticipated that Karen would be part of her plan, but she would have to cross that bridge when it was time. Katrina left her house every morning looking like a church girl. She had fifteen minutes to change before heading to her homeroom. She would disappear from the homeroom teacher's sight and head straight to the bathroom to transform herself to "Ms. Thang." She didn't just have Henry to deal with, but she now had the other boys who started to take notice of her curves and beauty. Henry was bringing out a rose among thorns. Katrina started to feel more confident and she started to like Henry even more. As much as Katrina liked Henry, that accidental kiss was the only kiss they ever shared. Henry respected her and she also respected herself. Katrina was not popular, but she was definitely noticeable.

As time went on, she even got Henry to trade in his Coke bottle glasses for some Gazelle's. The Gazelle glasses were also made famous by the group Run DMC. One of the rappers, DMC, wore those glasses. Henry was a different guy and he also started to adopt a new personality. He started to get irritated by Katrina because she wouldn't make out with him. All the respect and the holding out was becoming an issue. Other girls at the school also started to notice Henry and he didn't know what to do with himself. The other girls were moving at a faster pace than Katrina. There was no way that she was going to put out just to keep up with the other girls. She was not that kind of girl. Word had also gotten around that Henry was buying clothes for Katrina. The other girls were definitely interested in Henry then. By the end of the second quarter that fall, Henry and Katrina were no longer friends. He had lost his virginity to this girl whom he spent all his money on. He even got a pregnancy scare from her.

After Henry, Katrina decided to leave the boys alone all together, especially after she heard about the pregnancy scare with Henry and the girl. The last thing she had ever wanted was to bring a baby home. Her parents would kick her out instantly. Katrina continued to wear the nice clothes that Henry got her and she tried her best to keep her sister from seeing them. She had also established a system where her clothes went into a separate plastic bag so that her mother could never discover her secret. Karen though was a little too curious for Katrina to think that she was going to get away with it for too long.

One day while doing the laundry, Karen noticed that Katrina was throwing a pair of jeans in the wash that looked awfully different than the jeans her father and brother would wear. "Whose jeans are those?" she asked Katrina. Playing the stupid role, Katrina answered, "What jeans?" Karen knew what she saw. "The pair of Jeans you just threw in the wash," she said. "Oh, you talking about Eddy's jeans," Katrina tried to lie. "Since when did Eddy start wearing Calvin Klein Jeans? I know mom and dad wouldn't spend that kind of money on clothes for any of us, so where did you get them?" she asked. "I don't know what you're talking about," Katrina said to her sister while looking away suspiciously. Karen moved closer to the washing machine for a closer inspection of the contents in it. She pulled out the pair of jeans and after a careful inspection, she realized her sister had been holding out on her. A deal was brokered right away. Katrina agreed to let Karen wear her perfume to school twice a week if Karen kept it a secret from her parents.

Though Karen was a few years younger than Katrina, she was almost as developed mentally. Katrina couldn't believe how her little sister was trying to play her. Karen was as smart a child as they come and she always found a way to use every situation to her advantage. There was never any sibling rivalry between Katrina and Karen. Katrina knew that Karen was daddy's little girl and she accepted that. She couldn't understand why her father was so distant from her, sometimes. The fact that paternity for Katrina had never been confirmed was never discussed or told to her, but there was definitely distance between Buck and her. There was no certainty as to whether he resented her or not, but he treated her very differently, as did her mother. It was as if Katrina had disrupted the perfect home.

Chapter 29
Buck and Esther

Buck had been wrestling with the idea of finding out if Katrina was his biological child for a long time, but he didn't want his wife to know about the struggle within himself. He would stand and look at his daughter in the distance and would shake his head as if to say, 'There's no way that child is mine'. Buck continued to struggle with that and it affected his relationship with his daughter. It shouldn't even have mattered whether or not she was biologically his. He was the one who raised her from birth. Also, if she was Mr. Jamison's biological child, that was also no fault of her own. Esther didn't understand why Buck couldn't just let go. They would argue about it over and over and Esther would have to relive the whole ordeal that she went through with her father. Those arguments usually sent Esther in a depressing funk for weeks at a time. They were nightmarish events in her life that she buried deep, and Buck was very insensitive to her feelings. All he cared about was his own ego. Had Esther not been a devoted wife, she would have left Buck a long time ago.

There were times when Esther looked at her husband and wondered if she even loved the man. More importantly, she would question whether a man like Buck was even worth loving. But, whatever resentment she felt towards her husband, the sight of her children would always alter her mood and decision to leave. Esther's children were the center of her world and she sacrificed her own happiness to make sure they were being raised right.

The constant arguments with Buck were taking a toll on their marriage as well as their personal lives. Neither Katrina nor Buck knew how to find a solution to their problems.

At birth, Katrina looked like any normal baby, but everyone thought she looked like Mr. Jamison. It was okay for people to think that at first, because everyone, including Buck, thought Esther was his biological daughter. After uncovering Mr. Jamison's little secret with Esther, Katrina's resemblance to him didn't sit well with Buck anymore. His curiosity about the beautiful little girl he had raised was eating away at him and he couldn't stop thinking about the reality. He created this emotional barricade when it came to Katrina, and she started to sense it very early on in life. Though Buck tried to act as normal a parent as he could towards Katrina, his interaction with Eddy and Karen highlighted his lack of emotion for his daughter. Katrina was very perceptive as a child, so she kept her distance. The only person who could've changed the situation was Esther, but she had taken on the submissive role from the time she married Buck.

Esther never maximized her potential because she married a man who wanted to keep her in her "place." A man who was ashamed of his own background and upbringing, Buck tried in many ways to break Esther down, but she could not be broken. Every time she was ready to give up, she found strength in her children. Buck had become a stranger whom she shared a house with. No compassion or love was ever exchanged between them. Esther had changed mode from lover/wife to survivor. She needed to survive for her children. The man she fell for had changed and she needed to adjust to the new Buck. She also started to change as a person and slowly, but surely, a different kind of growth started taking place with Esther.

Still a devoted wife, Esther never thought about being with another man. Cheap thrills weren't her thing and sex had become so mundane with Buck that she lacked interest in it all together. Esther's only friends were the ladies from her church whose clothes she made. These women never discussed their family affairs outside of their homes, but they could see that Esther was not a happy woman. She was often invited to the women's retreat, organized by the ladies at the church, but Buck felt threatened by the idea of other women corrupting his wife's mind. He never allowed her to go, and to keep the peace at home, she never went. Esther's friends didn't dare talk about their sex lives because it was taboo. Poor Esther would be kept in the dark and she would never experience a sexually fulfilled life. It wasn't just Esther; Buck also never had a sexually fulfilled life. He only did what he thought was right sexually. Back then, it wasn't about pleasing the woman for most men. Buck had never been a gigolo and finding his wife, the one woman he ever loved, was good enough for him. The marriage could've worked a lot better if Buck had learned to express his love to his wife and children.

The issue with Katrina would linger on, but Buck never had enough guts to find out the truth. Over time, he had come to accept that she was his child and no one could change that. Still, his actions towards her never changed. The lack of affection continued, but he believed he was being a good father. Esther also never forced the issue because she didn't really know what to do about it.

Chapter 30
The Church

Buck and Esther were becoming more religious by the day. Each time they prayed, God would answer their prayers. They adored their pastor at church because he was a very charismatic, smooth talker who related well to his congregation. Pastor Chambers grew up around religion all of his life. He had inherited the word of God from his father who was also a pastor. The man had mastered his craft and he could have made an atheist believe in the existence of God after a sermon. It always seemed as if Pastor Chambers was talking directly to the Johnson family every Sunday. The issues that the family was going through were discussed openly in front of the congregation without having to personally tell the pastor about their problems. Esther and Buck couldn't understand it. It was as if God was talking to them through the pastor every single Sunday. The pastor was shining the light on their most intimate problems. It helped them see things clearer. The pastor's words also started to bring the family closer.

Whenever Esther felt like she was at the end of the rope in her marriage, she would hear from her pastor how a wife's devotion to her husband was the core of every marriage and how a man couldn't be well-adjusted without the support of his wife. The pastor even talked about how the husbands should make an effort to satisfy their wives in the bedroom. "Oh no, it ain't all about us, fellas. God didn't create this great thing called love just for the joy of men. Women have to be included in this too, fellas. Sex is sacred, but it has to be good for both of you. Can I get an Amen?" the pastor asked. All the women in the congregation were on their feet, yelling and screaming for deliverance from their selfish husbands. The pastor was clearly making a point to the men. There were whispers of Jezebels being in the church and the pastor understood that it could've been created through lack of satisfaction. "Love is not about jumping on top of your wife for five minutes and thinking everything is well and good. No it's not. Your wife has needs to and you better make sure those needs are met because church members are not immune to infidelity," the pastor told them. The women were once again on their feet, but Esther never once got up to cheer on the pastor like the rest of the women. The look on Buck's face was enough to kill. He knew he hadn't been a good lover to his wife. He never even thought about her satisfaction when he made "love" to her, but now he was being called out by his pastor, a man he respected. Buck had better start to change things in the bedroom for his wife.

Pastor Chambers also preached about the women who came to church dressing inappropriately. He didn't welcome churchgoers who wore pants to church. He didn't want to see any cleavage. He didn't like to see form fitting dresses on women and he didn't like married women who flirted with other men. Even though he talked to the church as a group, the individuals he reached through his sermons knew exactly that he was addressing them. When he talked about too much cleavage in the church, many women would inconspicuously try to button up their blouses. The women with tight dresses would throw on a jacket, and tears would start falling from the eyes of the Jezebels. The pastor was very far-reaching and effective.

Pastor Chambers didn't leave any stone unturned. He also talked about the right way for parents to rear their children. Children were expected to listen to their parents and the parents were supposed to be the guide, nurturers, as well as the provider for their children. The expectation for the children was that they would go to school and excel and the parents were supposed to provide the support they needed. Pastor Chambers made it very clear to the children of the church that premarital sex was unacceptable. Anybody from his church who was having premarital sex would be kicked out upon finding evidence that such actions had taken place. He also placed the responsibility squarely on the shoulders of the parents to talk to their children about sex. "They are children. You can't expect them to have all the information they need about sex without discussing it with them. You can't complain about becoming a grandmother at the age of thirty-five when you never talked to your teenage son or daughter about sex. Where are they supposed to get that information, from their friends?" That particular Sunday Pastor Chambers' sermon was right on point and on time. Buck and Esther had never talked to Katrina about sex even though she was now a teenager. Pastor Chambers had forced the issue upon them, but they didn't apply his lesson.

Peer pressure was also one of the subjects that Pastor Chambers talked about. He urged parents to talk to their children about the issue of fitting in. "When these children go to school, they are on their own. They get ridiculed for dressing a certain way that others may not particularly find attractive or popular. They might be a target because they choose to abstain from sex. They might be made fun of because of their religion. You, as parents, need to talk to your children about their individuality in a world filled with filth and indecency. You can't rely on the church or school to raise your children. That is your responsibility as a parent. The communication lines between you and your children should always be open," the pastor told the church. Again, Pastor Chambers was talking directly to Mr. and Mrs. Johnson. They needed to talk to their daughter about all of these issues, but they didn't feel it was necessary because it should've been understood.

The church wasn't just a place of worship for the Johnson family; it had also become a sanctuary. It was a place where they found answers to their problems, a place where light was shed, a place where they found counseling, a place where they felt connected to God, a place where they found direction in life, and a place where happiness lived. The Johnson family attended church three times a week; twice for service and once a week for Bible study. The whole family went to church and they were all supposed to live and abide by the word of God.

Chapter 31
Growing Pains

Since Katrina and Henry "broke up," Henry had become more popular than ever. With popularity came the painstaking chore of lying to live up to the "cool" reputation. Henry by then had lost his virginity to a young lady who was just too hot for her own good. During a conversation among his friends one day, Henry felt the need to outdo his friend by lying about the salacious details of a supposedly sexual encounter that involved Katrina. "Man, I was doing everything to her. I did it from behind, on the bed and even in the living room while her mom was at work," said one of Henry's friends about another girl in the school. "Did you ever get a piece of Katrina?" the friend than asked. Henry caved under pressure. Instead of giving his friends a true account of what happened between him and Katrina during their friendship, he decided to fabricate a tantalizing story that would make him the talk of the school, which would ultimately lead back to his neighborhood where Katrina also lived.

"Hell yeah I got a piece of that," Henry lied to his friends. "It was good too. I was her first man. I also taught her how to do me right," he continued to lie. The only time Henry ever kissed Katrina was that time when she turned her head and their lips met accidentally. There was no other time. As the conversation progressed, his friends tried to solicit more details from Henry. Feeling cornered and pressured, Henry started concocting more of his fairytale relationship with Katrina, making himself look good, while she looked like a little tramp. "She went down on me, bro," he lied to his friends again. Back then, one of the worst things a black girl could do was to perform oral sex on her boyfriend. That was sacred stuff and black girls just didn't do that. That lie catapulted Henry's rep to almost a jock, while Katrina's reputation took a dive. "She did that, yo? Dammmmmn. I need to try to get me a piece of that," said one of his friends, thinking that Katrina was easy. "She ain't my girl no more. Go for yours, man," Henry told him nonchalantly. His friend would never get a chance to "go for his" because Katrina was never that type of girl.

Word would eventually get back to Katrina about the whole incident and she confronted Henry about it in a private meeting. Of course, Henry denied that he had ever told his friends any part of the story. However, the part of

the story where Katrina had performed oral sex on Henry
had gotten back to her neighborhood and her parents heard
about it. Buck almost beat the crap out of Katrina when she
got home that day. He was so angry; he didn't even bother
asking her any questions. He smacked her dead in the face
when she entered the house. Katrina was scared and had no
idea why her dad smacked her. "What, you the little tramp
of the neighborhood now? You're going around not only
having sex with these boys, but you're doing things that not
even your mother and I would do," Buck told her angrily.
Katrina knew exactly what her father was talking about. She
also realized at that point that Buck had not been getting any
oral treatment from his wife. No wonder he was always so
frustrated. Anyway, Katrina thought about calling 911 after
her father smacked her, while her mother looked on, but she
also realized she didn't want to be caught dead in anybody's
foster home either. Whatever beating she was gonna get, she
would have to deal with it. Realizing what he had done out
of anger, Buck walked out of the house before hitting
Katrina again. He was fuming.

Katrina tried telling her mother that it was all a lie,
but her mother didn't want to hear it. The rumor had been
planted and they thought it was true. Katrina wanted so
badly to go to Henry's house with her parents to confront

him, but his family had moved to another part of Hyde Park by then. Buck would go on to hold this incident against his daughter for a while, but Katrina didn't make things any easier on her parents.

Buck had made it clear to his daughters that he didn't want them to ever wear denim jeans. His wife knew that she was not allowed to buy them certain kinds of clothing because they were forbidden. Katrina had gotten a taste of the attention she received from those clothes that Henry bought her, and she couldn't get enough. Spurning the idea of not wearing those clothes was the farthest thing from her mind. She continued to enjoy wearing the denim jeans, mini skirts, halter tops and other racy clothes that she also started to purchase for herself with her allowance.

One day Katrina made the mistake of boarding the school bus wearing those jeans on the way home from school. Unfortunately, she was spotted by a church member who thought it would be funny if she mentioned it to her mother at church the following Sunday. Katrina had planned to change back into her regular clothes on the back of the bus that day, which she did. Her parents had no reason to be suspicious of her until that lady convincingly told her mother that she was certain she had seen Katrina wearing a tight pair of jeans with a sweater exposing her shoulders.

Esther immediately went into Katrina's closet without saying anything to her and started looking for the clothes. Katrina caught a break that day because she had brought all of her clothes to school with her after the lady screamed out her name to make sure it was her that she saw. Katrina ignored the voice that was calling her and quickly changed into her regular clothes after boarding the bus. She never made eye contact with the woman from the church.

Katrina found no reason for her parents to forbid her from wearing certain clothing items. Every kid at her school was wearing some of the most popular brands. She didn't care about exposing her navel, as most of the other girls did, but she wanted to start wearing clothes that accentuated her figure. It gave her confidence in a world where she was seen as an outcast. Katrina continued to struggle with the consequences she faced if she ever got caught, but she stuck with the clothes for the greater good, which was her image at school. Her parents didn't have to endure the teasing by the other students at school, she did. She figured that she would be careful enough and they would never find out about what she was doing. Her mother never brought up the subject because she had no evidence of clothing to confront Katrina with. From that point on, Katrina was careful not to bring any of her clothes home. She started taking them to the dry cleaner located a couple of blocks from her school. It was an elaborate plan to avoid getting caught. While Katrina's plan may have been working for many months, Karen wasn't as careful. Karen was a little more daring and she enjoyed the attention she was getting from the boys at her school. She was very feisty for a young girl and the young boys started to take notice. The perfume that Katrina allowed her to wear twice a week now became the norm. Karen was always showing off to her friends about how good she smelled. One day, she forgot that her dad was planning to pick her up from school. She was about to board the school bus while still wearing the perfume on her neck and wrists, when her dad showed up to pick her up. She forgot to wash it off in the bathroom as planned. When she got in her father's car, he noticed the smell on her immediately. He quickly got out of his car and dragged his daughter by the ear for a beating, but he stopped because there were too many people watching him. He was so upset that all the kids on the school bus were looking at him in dead silence. No one even knew why he reacted the way he did. Karen knew she was in trouble and she had better start thinking of a way to get out of it.

Buck didn't want his kids to wear anything fashionable that would bring more attention than they needed. There was silence in the car during the drive home. Karen just knew that her father was about to beat the crap out of her. While she was sitting in the car with tears flowing down her face, she asked her dad, "Are you even going to ask me why I'm wearing the perfume, daddy?" Buck almost reached across the seat to smack his daughter in the mouth, as a knee-jerk reaction from his anger. He knew his wife would be angry if he got the Department of Social Services involved in their lives again, so he chilled. "Daddy, I'm gonna tell you why anyway." Karen had already thought of her lie and she knew how to use her little innocent voice and face to get over on her dad. "Daddy, we were doing show and tell in class today and one of the girls brought a bottle of perfume to school as her item. She started spraying the perfume and we all got a little of it on us. I didn't really have no choice, daddy," she said while sulking. Lucky for her, Buck didn't reach over to look in her bag to find out what item she brought to school for show and tell. He sure would have found the same bottle of perfume in her bag.

When Karen and her dad finally made it home, Katrina's heart almost sank down to her feet. She thought

Karen had sold her out when she walked through the door wearing the perfume with her father in tow. It was a strong smelling perfume that Henry had purchased for Katrina. A quick confusing signal with her head towards Katrina to tell her that everything was cleared couldn't be read by Katrina. She was scared and just knew that Buck was about to go grab his belt and let them have it. "Go to the bathroom and wash this smell off of you," Buck yelled at Karen. Katrina was still a little confused about the events. She was waiting for her father to ask Karen questions about the origin of the perfume, but he never did. She followed Karen into her room and Karen explained to her the lies that she had told her father in the car. Instead of being happy about being cleared of the situation, Katrina was angry. She was angry because she knew that her father would have never given her a break. The favoritism that her father had shown towards Karen since she was a little girl was still prevalent. Katrina was starting to despise her father for it.

Katrina's defiant behavior was about to change her whole life as she knew it. She finally made it out of eighth grade to the ninth grade. By then, she saw boys as nothing but pests because of what happened with Henry. She had trusted him as a friend and he betrayed her trust. She didn't want anything to do with any of the boys in her class. She kept to herself most of the time and she also stopped wearing the fashionable clothes to school because Karen had been caught wearing perfume. She knew for sure that she would get caught one day and the consequences for her would be very different than Karen. Katrina reverted back to her books and wanted to focus more on her studies. She in no way wanted to upset her parents, but she would still defy them every now and then, as most teenagers do to parents.

There was an open field near Katrina's house, which most people used as a shortcut to get home quicker, her parents had warned her about the shortcut. They specifically told her to stay clear of the field because there was an increase in crime that took place on that field. Buck was adamant and made sure he reiterated the fact that he didn't want Katrina to walk through that field. However, some days Katrina would feel so tired that the field seemed to be the only option to get home quickly. She figured she could walk through the field during the day because she would be safe. She didn't walk through there often, but she did it enough to increase her chances of getting attacked.

When this boy named Jose started meeting Katrina at her bus stop every morning, she didn't think much of it. Though she found him annoying, she never said anything to her parents about him. At first, Jose seemed like he was looking for a friend, but Katrina was not interested. She brushed him off on more than one occasion, but he kept pestering her. Finally she started to respond to him and before she knew it, Jose was waiting for her at the bus stop everyday. They had even walked through the field together once. She also revealed to him that her parents didn't want her to walk through that field. Katrina, over time, started to trust Jose more than she should have. She never saw him as a threat or as somebody who would harm her. She had gotten past the Henry situation and she was moving on.

Chapter 32
The Neighborhood

As more black and Hispanic families started to move into Hyde Park, the big white migration started to take place. White folks were selling their homes for less than market value because they didn't want to live around a bunch of Negroes and Hispanics. It was a good thing for the minority homeowners because they formed a neighborhood watch and they started becoming closer as neighbors. It was the "it takes a village to raise a child" mentality. Every neighbor on that street knew the kids who lived on that street and who their parents were. The neighborhood had changed drastically over time. Suddenly there were people hanging out on the front porches of homes all over the street. Buck wasn't too happy that people started to invade his neighborhood. Of course, it was an upwardly mobile street for up and coming African-American and Hispanic families who had reached their dreams of home ownership in a decent neighborhood, but some of those kids started to bring the bad element from wherever they came from right along with them.

The value of Buck's home had quadrupled since he bought it and he enjoyed the fact that his kids were safe, and that he didn't have to worry about his home being broken into. As the Hyde Park section of Boston started to attract more minority people, the worse the police response to incidents became. When Buck first bought the house, it took the cops less than five minutes to respond to any kind of call. It didn't matter if it was somebody's cat stuck in a tree or a domestic quarrel between a couple; they responded quickly. The demographics had changed, and so did the cops' attitude. Now, the walk to the bus stop wasn't as fun anymore for Katrina. Guys were whistling at her and making lewd comments at the same time, and she didn't know how to respond to it.

Katrina started feeling more uncomfortable as the days passed and when Jose showed up to befriend her, she was just happy that he had become a safety net every morning while she waited for the bus. Most of the guys on the block knew who he was, so they didn't really bother Katrina anymore after he started claiming her as his friend. Jose kept pushing for more, but Katrina stood her ground. After a while she almost started to feel sorry for him because he was already out of high school and there he was, trying to talk to a high school freshman. Katrina hadn't been exposed to guys like Jose, so she didn't know the potential danger she was in.

Chapter 33
Nowhere To Run

Buck and his wife had tried their best to raise the perfect family. They were fortunate enough to have a brother like BJ who was willing to give them a head start in life financially. Buck and Esther both had difficult lives and upbringings, but neither of them ever sought help to deal with the trauma they had gone through in their lives. The great escape appeared to be God, a good job, a home and a family. If it were that easy, most dysfunctional families would never repeat the abusive cycle that they have had to deal with for many generations.

Buck and Esther had seen and experienced ignorance most of their lives, and in the process they became ignorant themselves. They were ignorant to many things, including the physical and sexual abuse that took place in their lives. In the Johnson case, it seemed as if they were destined for many things, but they never took control of their destiny. They never made their problems a priority, thus their children grew up having to deal with the same issues. Katrina, Eddy and Karen were given better opportunities than their parents, but the environment was always the same no matter where they went. The parents carried their issues around with them and nothing was ever resolved. There were no great examples of parenting in either of their lives and their children would go on to suffer the consequences.

Esther had escaped one form of abuse when she left her father's house to marry Buck, but she also entered a new phase of psychological abuse without realizing it. Though Buck had never raised his hands to her, he was a controlling man who didn't know any other way to interact with his family. He had grown up watching his dad control his family with an iron fist, and sort of adopted his dad's ways without even knowing it. Buck wanted to be a better man, but there was no one around to teach him a better way to do things. He tried to develop his own way, and as a result, there was a new type dysfunction in his family. Maybe the lack of a formal education had something to do with the way the Johnson family continued to function.

Unfortunately, Buck and his wife never took the time to reflect on their lives. Perhaps they never had the time to reflect because survival became a task from the very beginning. They each had to deal with so many issues before they got married, but they failed to address them, so when they got together it was a complete mess. A mess they never even anticipated.

Sometimes Esther wished she had taken the time to get to know Buck better, to learn about his life, but it was too late. While looking for an escape from agony, she found herself in a lot more pain. The whole concept of marriage as Esther knew it was very different than what she had been experiencing, and most of the time she had to turn to her offspring to find enough strength to stay in her marriage. Buck was no different. He had become a stoic man and also a man of pride and dignity, but where did his pride and dignity come from? He was not raised with any. It was especially hard for Buck to become a strong-willed man when his father almost broke his spirit as a boy.

Every night the Johnson couple did the only thing that they felt comfortable and confident doing; they prayed to God for the safety of their children, good health and prosperity. Whether that will ever be the case, only time will tell for the Johnson family.

The End

Please check out the sequel to this book called

Neglected Souls

Sample chapter
Neglected Souls
Chapter 1
Stolen Innocence

Katrina and her children were very close in age. She was just fourteen years old when her daughter, Nina, was born and sixteen years old when her son, Jimmy, was born. Neither father was involved in the kids' lives. As a matter of fact, the fathers were unknown to both children. Katrina could've never told Jimmy who his father was anyway. She would have had too much explaining to do. Nina's father on the other hand, was a man of Hispanic descent who had sexually violated Katrina. He was an older boy from the neighborhood where Katrina grew up.

When Katrina found out she was pregnant with Nina a month after she had been raped, she told her very religious parents what had happened but they did not believe her. There was a rumor going around the neighborhood that Katrina had slept with another boy in the neighborhood. That rumor ultimately tarnished her reputation with her own parents. Once she revealed to them that she was pregnant, it basically confirmed the rumor that she was promiscuous.

Katrina's parents never gave her a chance to explain how she was impregnated against her will through a rape. Her account of the event did not matter to her parents. Her parents turned their backs on her and called her all kinds of trifling names and immediately kicked her out of the house. She left with her supposed bundle of joy in her stomach and never went back home. Katrina gave birth to Nina all alone in the hospital. At the age of fourteen years old, she had to find a way to provide financially and emotionally for her daughter.

Katrina was a loner in high school who spent most of her time studying, but she would always get giddy and nervous around boys. She didn't know how to react to advances from the boys and shied away from most kids her age because they were always making fun of her. Jose saw Katrina's alienation from her peers as an opportunity to try to befriend her. Jose was about five years older than Katrina; he had just graduated from high school that past June and was waiting to be shipped out to the military.

It was early October when Jose had his first conversation with Katrina. Jose Ramirez was a short and chubby man who was about a sandwich away from being obese. He was no taller than five ft five inches and weighed about one hundred and seventy five pounds. He had spiked hair and enough pimples on his face to earn him the nickname "Pizza Face" back in high school. He was also an abrasive man who could turn a sweet old lady into a modern day bitch. He was rude and had the confidence of a super hero around younger women. Nobody could tell Jose he wasn't God's gift to young and impressionable women. Around people his age, he clammed up in a shell that nobody could open.

Jose had so many different complexes it would take a lifetime to list them all. However, the one apparent one was his Napoleon complex to compensate for his lack of height. He felt the need to dominate young impressionable people around where he lived. He didn't have any friends his age. He would always try to gather the younger kids on his block to tell them glorified, fictitious stories about himself in high school. Most of the kids figured he was lying because he would always stop talking when the older guys from the neighborhood who went to school with him showed up. He was a super hero in his own mind.

Katrina lived with her parents in Hyde Park, which was a small suburb of Boston, near the Dedham line. Back in the seventies and early eighties, the city of Boston provided those ugly yellow cheese buses for transportation to all students who lived more than five miles away from their school. Every student who rode a school bus had an assigned stop to board the bus every morning. It was usually a block or two and no more from a student's home.

Because Katrina lived so far away in Hyde Park and her school was located near Fenway Park, she was assigned a school bus. Katrina boarded her bus two blocks away from her house every morning at 6:35 AM in order to get to school by 7:20 AM and the bus would drop her off at 2:30 in the afternoon everyday. It was a routine schedule and Jose had figured out exactly how to talk to Katrina without her parents finding out. He would go to her bus stop every afternoon to wait for her so he could walk her home. At first, she was irritated by him and didn't really pay him any attention. But his persistence finally paid off two weeks later when she finally opened her mouth to ask him why he continued to bother her everyday even though she ignored him.

He became cocky and told her that he knew that she would eventually come around to her senses. Jose was the type of guy who took a turn down as an invitation to come-on to a woman. In his own mind, she had always wanted to talk to him. However, as time went by, Katrina started to see a different side of Jose. She saw a desperately confused young man who was seeking the approval of his friends, and their personalities were pretty similar. They became friends and she made it clear to him that it was all that they could be. The thought of anything more never even crossed her mind.

Kissing boys was the furthest thing from Katrina's mind when she entered high school early that fall. She still saw boys as pests whose jobs were to make fun of people all day. She was grossed out by the idea of someone shoving his tongue down her throat to kiss her. One can only imagine how appalled she was on the day Jose tried to steal a kiss from her. He came out of nowhere, without any warning, and planted a big wet kiss on her. It was literally wet because Katrina's mouth remained closed while he was trying to stick his tongue in her mouth. The first word out her mouth was "yuck!" as she ran away from Jose. She couldn't believe he had physically violated her like that after just two weeks of befriending her. She realized that she should not have let down her guard around him so soon. She ran the whole way home hysterically angry.

Katrina was never attracted to Jose and found his body odor to be rather offensive, but she never felt comfortable enough with him to tell him. Katrina had set the parameters on their friendship from the beginning and Jose had crossed the line. She couldn't forgive him and did not want to forgive him for what he had done. From that day on, she believed their friendship was over and there was no way she was going to change her mind about it.

A week had passed and by this time Jose had become repulsive to her. He was still relentless in his pursuit to rekindle the friendship he and Katrina once shared. She wanted none of it and Jose's ego was crushed. Jose wasn't ready to deal with another rejection, especially by a young, impressionable chick. The day Jose planted the kiss on Katrina's lips, he had hoped for it to be this fairytale situation he had dreamed up in his mind for weeks. He never factored in the fact that it took two people to tangle. He felt like an idiot standing there when she ran away from him after his romantic attempt at kissing her the week before. Jose wanted to know the reason why Katrina had not grown to like him. She enjoyed his jokes and they formed somewhat of a friendship.

Katrina was not a rude or open person, so she kept all her feelings inside. She was rather timid while Jose was clueless. He was always projecting his feelings onto other people without communicating with them. He found out the hard way that his advances were not welcomed. Katrina ignored him for two weeks and for two weeks he kept trying to get her attention. One particular week, he went and dropped a rose on her front porch every morning with a note saying he missed their friendship. She never responded to his effort and Jose was once again embarrassed.

Katrina had never told anyone about the incident with Jose. She didn't have any friends to confide in and her parents who were very old fashioned weren't the kind of parents she could go to with boy issues. They tried as much as they could to shield their kids from the sins of the world or what the bible made them believe to be sins. Katrina was the eldest of three children; she had a younger brother and a younger sister that followed. Katrina was five years older than her brother and seven years older than her sister. Her parents had set high expectations for all their kids and if they didn't do as they were told they were shunned.

Katrina always had a hard time getting up for church on Sundays and she had made her parents late for service on numerous occasions. She had earned the reputation of a rebel early from her parents. She once told her parents that she didn't want to go to church because God could care less if she prayed in church or at home. Her parents were furious that she had talked back to them in such a manner. She was grounded for a week. Katrina's parents didn't want her to have a negative influence on her younger siblings. They tried as much as they could to keep her siblings away from her. Katrina's parents had started to develop preconceived feelings of mistrust towards their daughter because she didn't agree with them all the time. They never took the time to get to know their daughter; instead, they became preoccupied with shielding their younger children from her. Katrina's parents never allowed her to be an adolescent.

Katrina's innocent, rebellious behavior was not at all innocent to her parents. Katrina's parents took their daughter's occasional defiance seriously. They had on numerous occasions made it clear to Katrina that they didn't want her walking through an abandoned field, located a block away from their house. And not a moment too soon, her younger brother had seen her cutting through the field from his bedroom window. He alerted his mother who saw Katrina doing exactly what they had told her not to do. When she got home, she was confronted and she lied about it. She had started to build a barrier of mistrust between her and her parents.

A neighbor once told her parents that they had seen her wearing jeans coming out of school. Her parents forbade Katrina from wearing pants. They were strict Christians and they didn't want their daughter to bend any of the Christian rules. Katrina was slowly becoming the black sheep of the family. She would buy clothes prohibited by her parents with her allowance and would carry them in her bag to school and change in the bathroom. The more they tried to control Katrina, the more she pushed their buttons and the more defiant she became.

Jose had it all planned in his head. He wanted to get Katrina back for rejecting him and he thought he came up with the perfect plan. It was a wonderful sunny Friday afternoon in the fall of 1984 and Jose was set to leave the following day for the army. He hadn't seen or bothered Katrina in weeks.

She was glad he was no longer pestering her about being his friend. However, on that fateful day, "Pizza Face" showed his ugly head once again. This time, Jose didn't go through the same routine at the bus stop; instead, he waited for Katrina about a block from her house.

As usual, Katrina defied her parents' orders and walked through the abandoned field as a short cut and Jose knew this. As she cut through the field, Jose approached her with a gun in his hand and told her to shut up or he would kill her as he put the gun to her head. He threw down her book bag then smacked her and knocked her down to the ground. On this day, when Jose confronted Katrina, she was wearing a long skirt that her mother had laid out on the bed for her the night before. While Katrina was on the ground, Jose covered her mouth with his left hand while lifting her skirt up with the gun in his right hand. He brought her skirt up to her waist then proceeded to rub the gun up and down her vagina through her underwear. In his sick mind, he kept telling her that she liked it and wanted more of it. Jose then pushed Katrina's underwear to the side with the gun then stuck it inside her vagina as she winced in pain.

Katrina was not sexually active and had never had any object in her vagina prior to this heinous incident. It hurt to have the barrel of a gun thrust inside of her. He went on about how he could blow her up and have her guts spill out by pulling the trigger while the gun was still inside of her. Katrina wanted to fight back but she couldn't; he got on top of her and overpowered her with his weight and the gun pressed against her head. The sorrow in her face could only be described as innocence lost. Tears ran down her face as she lay on the ground with her eyes closed.

A few minutes had passed and Katrina was no longer responding to Jose's sick remarks, he grew angrier and he decided that raping her would be the ultimate revenge. He pulled her panties to the side, rammed his short penis inside her vagina while holding the gun in her mouth. He must've humped her for about a minute before he came. When he got up he told her that he would kill her if she told anybody and would kill her brother and sister as well. He left her lying on the grass powerless and ashamed.

She blamed herself for the whole incident because her parents had told her many times not to walk through the field. Other women had been assaulted there at all hours of the day in the past. Poor Katrina didn't even have the strength to get up from the ground to walk the rest of the way home. She felt no longer pristine and had lost her virginity to a despicable rapist.

She finally mustered the courage to get up after about forty-five minutes and headed home. When she got home, she went straight to the shower to wash off Jose's dirty paws and sexual aggression he'd forced upon her. After she got out of the shower, she went to her room where she sobbed for the rest of the night. She did not eat dinner nor did she speak to anybody about the incident. Her parents didn't even bother checking up on her. Her parents were old school and they didn't know how to talk to their daughter. No attempt was made to reach out to Katrina and she felt isolated and alone in a house full of people. Katrina felt she had contributed to the rape because she had defied her parents' orders to avoid the abandoned field. She dealt with her dilemma the best way she could that Friday night and that day she just wanted to sleep away the whole experience.

After trying to sleep her problems away for twelve hours, Katrina woke up on Saturday afternoon feeling worn out. With no one to talk to about the situation, Katrina contemplated suicide. She wanted to pour a glass of Clorox mixed with milk down her throat to end her life. She went downstairs to the washroom in the basement and started pouring Clorox in a cup. When her little brother came down looking for her to play hide and seek, she decided that it was not worth it. She took one look at him and smiled and went back upstairs to play with him for a little while. But her brother only provided temporary relief from her problems.

Soon after, Katrina started thinking about the whole ordeal again. She became withdrawn and went back upstairs and locked herself in her room. Katrina didn't eat anything that day and she was a nervous wreck. Every little noise only increased her paranoia. Finally, her younger sister came knocking on her bedroom door that evening to see how she was doing and why she hadn't talked to her all day. Her sister loved to play with Katrina's long and thick curly hair. She came in the room with a comb in hand and wanted to play hairdresser with Katrina, but Katrina had a pounding headache. She told her sister it wasn't a good time to come back later. Her sister sadly left the room.

It was Sunday morning when Katrina was awakened by the pounding knock of her father's fist on her bedroom door.

She had once again overslept and only had a few minutes to get ready for church. Her father told her she had five minutes to get ready or she would have to catch a bus to the church and meet them there. Katrina didn't have the strength to ride the bus that day, so she quickly got up, took a quick shower and threw on the first dress she could lay her hands on.

On the way to church, all Katrina kept thinking about was how God must've punished her for disobeying her parents' directives. She started feeling guilty and thought she deserved what happened to her. She could not wait to get into church to get on her knees and ask God for forgiveness and the strength to deal with her problems. Katrina was quiet the whole way to church and everyone in the car on that particular day seemed somber.

They arrived at the church just in time to catch the pastor announce his sermon topic of abortion and premarital sex. It was as if the gods were watching Katrina. The pastor talked about how the female body is a temple and it is up to women to protect it and at no time should they allow temptation to get the best of them. He also went on to preach that even in extreme cases of rape it is still considered immoral to abort a baby.

Katrina sat through church service for three hours; listening to this man babble on about how women have to take the initiative to protect themselves from men. The whole service felt weird to Katrina because she was raped two days ago and now this pastor was preaching about fornication and abortion. When it was time for prayer, Katrina knelt down and asked God to forgive her for the times she had disobeyed her parents and she promised she would never do that again. But she also asked God why he didn't protect her from Jose.

She left church feeling puzzled that day, thinking that although her parents were overly religious, their prayers did not even protect her from an attacking perpetrator. Katrina started questioning everything, thinking that maybe they didn't include her in their prayers when they prayed. During the ride back home, her father reiterated everything that the pastor had talked about to his children. Her father went on and on about how women who wore tight jeans and miniskirts were doing themselves a disservice. All was quiet in the car when her father was talking and that only increased her loneliness and Katrina felt even more ashamed about what happened to her.

Katrina's parents acted like slavery never ended. Mrs. Johnson was very submissive to her husband and she adopted a few of his bad habits in the process. Mr. Johnson's word in the house was bond and no one was allowed to question his decisions. There was loyalty in their home, but it was rare for the parents to express love to each other and their children. It was understood that the whole family was loved, but daddy didn't know how to express it.

The Johnsons only had a sixth grade education and were forced to join the workforce when they were very young to help support their very large families. Mr. Johnson grew up in a household with fifteen children and a single mother while Mrs. Johnson had ten siblings in a single-family household growing up. The Johnson's had continued to follow a negative cycle that existed in their families for many generations. Their grandparents were ex-slaves who were forbidden to express love to their children and they passed those traits on to their offspring. The Johnson's believe that children were to listen to their parents and that was the only opinion that mattered.

Sample Chapter

Hoodfellas II
American Gangster

Chapter 1

Haiti's clear skies, warm sunshine and inviting winds offer the perfect accommodating situation to explore the country's natural splendor. It's undiscovered, pristine trails, and foothills present the best opportunity for a serene bike ride. An abundance of outdoor opportunities reside in the back mountains of this precious island. The effervescent mood of the people is welcoming and embracing. With plenty of open spaces and green pasture for miles to come, warm climate and plenty of fresh Caribbean air, it's inexcusable to spend too much time indoor on this wonderful island. All of this aura brought a new sense of being to Deon Campbell. He felt rejuvenated when he first arrived in Haiti.

Deon thought he had left his criminal and troubled past behind and was hoping to start anew in a place where nobody knew his name. The fresh Caribbean air hit his face the minute he stepped off the cruise ship, and he just knew that the lifestyle of the rich and infamous was calling his name. With enough money to buy part of the island, Deon wouldn't have any financial worries until his calling from God. On the drive to Jean Paul's mansion caravan-style with a Toyota Sequoia ahead of him with armed security men and another Land Cruiser jeep filled with additional armed security men behind the limousine, Deon's mind was free to think about how he would miss his best friends and buddies, Short Dawg and No neck while riding in the air conditioned, long stretch limousine with his new friend, Jean Paul, and his entourage. He wanted to exact revenge on Short Dawg and No Neck's murderers and he would spend as much money it would take to make sure their killers don't live to see another day.

"I see you're a serious man and you're serious about your business," Deon said to Jean Paul as he sipped on a bottle of water while Jean Paul sipped on cognac. "In this country, you have to be. Don't let all the armed security intimidate you, it's a way of life here in Haiti," Jean Paul told him. An additional limousine also followed with all the luggage and money that Deon had to carry to Haiti with him. One of Deon's men rode with the second limousine driver. Keeping his eyes on the prize was very important and Deon didn't hide the fact that he wanted to know where his money was at all times. "I can't help but notice the worried look on your face, your money is fine. I have some of the best security men that Haiti has to offer..." and before the words could escape Jean Paul's mouth, gunfire erupted and bullets were flying everywhere from both sides of the road. A group of men emerged with machine guns as they attempted to stop the caravan so they could rob the crew. Deon had been in battle before, but this shit was ten times more than he had ever seen and he didn't know if Jean Paul had set him up or if they were just being robbed. "This fucking Haitian posse bullshit again!" Jean Paul screamed out loud. "Don't worry about a thing. All the cars are bullet proof down to the tires, but we're gonna teach these bastards a lesson, so they'll never fuck with me again. In each of those little compartments next to the button to lock your door is a nickel plated 9 millimeter, you guys are free to take out as many of them as possible. Their lives are worth shit here," he told them. At the push of a button, Jean Paul opened his compartment and pulled out two loaded .45 Lugar's. He cracked opened his window, and aimed at the pedestrian robbers. The crew of almost 20 men stood no chance as Jean Paul and his men returned fire with high powered guns from the barricaded bullet proof windows of the vehicles. A raid in Vietnam wouldn't even compare to the massacre that went on for about 2 minutes. After all the men were down, Jean Paul got out of the car to make sure that none of them had any breath left in them. It was like a firing squad as his men went around unloading bullets in the bodies lying across the pavement, ensuring that every one of the robbers was dead! The last crawling survivor received two bullets in each knee and one to the head before revealing that he was part of the Haitian posse located in the slums of Cite Soleil, the most dangerous slum in Port-Au-Prince, Haiti.

Even the United Nations guards, who are sent to monitor the situation in Haiti, were too afraid to go into Cite Soleil. The Haitian police feared confrontation in the slums because they were always outgunned and very few officers who went against the gang lived to tell about it another day. Jean Paul had been a target ever since his arrival in Haiti because he never hid his lavish lifestyle. A brash former drug dealer who grew up in the States, and was deported back to his homeland some twenty years later, he was not accustomed to the Haitian lifestyle or Haitian culture. After arriving in Haiti, Jean Paul had to learn his culture all over again. Americans like to say they're hungry enough to go do something drastic to feed their family, but in Haiti, those people literally lived it. Forced to eat dirt cookies due to lack of food, money and other resources, these gang members were tired of being hungry and anybody who got in their paths will pay the price for a better life, or better yet, food.

Many Haitian immigrants left Haiti with the hopes to one day go back to their homeland to help with the financial, economical, social infrastructure as well as democratic leadership. However, many of them usually find that what they left behind some twenty to thirty years ago has changed to the worst Haiti that they have ever seen. Since the departure of Baby Doc, Haiti has taken a turn for the worst and the economic climate in Haiti has forced many of its delinquents to become criminals of the worst kinds. While in the United States poor families are offered food stamps, subsidized housing and other economic relief by the government; in Haiti, relief only comes in the form of money sent to those who have relatives who live abroad. Those without relatives abroad suffer the worst kind of inhumane treatment, hunger, malnourishment, social inadequacies and the worst health.

To top off an already problematic situation, many of the Haitian politicians are unconscionable thieves who look to fill their pockets while the country is in dire need of every imaginable resource possible, including, but not limited to jobs, healthcare, social programs, education, clean water, deforestation, land development, any kind of industry and so on. Many of the elected officials offer promises, but rarely deliver on the promises after taking office. Most of the time, they become puppets of the United States government and in turn, look for their own self-interest instead of the interest of the people. Deon had no idea what he was stepping into and on the surface it appeared as if he would lead a peaceful life in the first Black republic of the world.

There's a price to be paid for freedom and winning a war against Napoleon's super French army with machetes and pure heart of warriors, the Haitians are definitely paying a price for it now. A brief history on the country was given to Deon and his crew by Jean Paul while on their three-hour drive to Jacmel from Port-Au-Prince where Jean Paul resided. Deon learned how Haiti, known back then as the pearl of the Antilles, has lost its luster and every resource it used to own due to deforestation. Coffee, sugarcane, cocoa and mangos are just a few of the natural resources and national products that the country used to offer the world, but most of it has evaporated because the government has not provided any assistance to the people to help them become self-sufficient in farming and land development. Security is one of the major reasons why foreign companies stay out of Haiti, and the government is not doing anything to bring back those companies as well as tourism, which helped the country thrive under the leadership of dirty old Papa Doc.

It was disheartening to Deon and his crew as they watched little kids running wild on the street digging through piles of trash looking for food along with the wild pigs and dogs on the side of the roads. Their faces reeked of pain, loneliness, hunger, starvation, malnutrition and hopelessness. Most of Deon's roughneck crew members were teary eyed as they watched this for almost two hours during the drive before hitting the scenic part of Haiti. Undeterred by the events that took place in the capital a few hours earlier, Deon ordered the driver to pull over in the center of St. Marc to hand out hundred dollar bills to a group of hungry children. The whole crew took part in handing out the money to the children who looked like they hadn't eaten a good meal since birth. Cindy took it especially hard as she was the only woman amongst the crew and Jean Paul didn't hide the fact that the minority two percent of white people in Haiti and another ten percent of mullatoes and people of mixed heritage controlled the wealth of Haiti.

It was evident who the wealthy people in Haiti were as they drove around in their frosty Range Rovers, Land Cruisers and other big name SUV's with their windows up as they navigate through the ghetto to rape the people of their wealth during the day while they rest their heads in their mansion in the Hills at night. The children rejoiced as Deon and the crew gave them enough money that would probably last them a whole month and more, to feed themselves and their families. Jean Paul was happy to see that his new friends sympathized with the people of Haiti, but he cautioned for them not to allow their kindness to become a habit as it could be detrimental to their livelihood.

It may not be Histeria Lane, but these desperate housewives are fed up with their neglecting husbands. Their sexual needs take precedence over the millions of dollars their husbands bring home every year to keep them happy in their affluent neighborhood. While their husbands claim to be hard at work, these wives are doing a little work of their own with the bedroom bandit. Is the bandit swift enough to evade these angry husbands?

In Stores!!

NEGLECTED SOULS

Motherhood and the trials of loving too hard and not enough frame this story...The realism of these characters will bring tears to your spirit as you discover the hero in the villain you never saw coming...

In Stores!!!

Jimmy and Nina continue to feel a void in their lives because they haven't a clue about their genealogical make-up. Jimmy falls victims to a life threatening illness and only the right organ donor can save his life. Will the donor be the bridge to reconnect Jimmy and Nina to their biological family? Will Nina be the strength for her brother in his time of need? Will they ever find out what really happened to their mother?

In Stores!!!

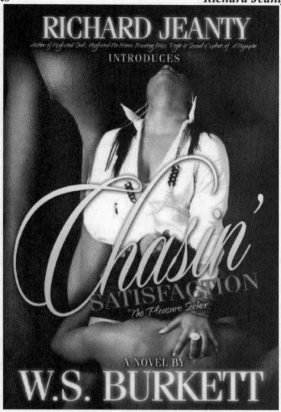

Betrayal, lust, lies, murder, deception, sex and tainted love frame this story... Julian Stevens lacks the ambition and freak ability that Miko looks for in a man, but she married him despite his flaws to spite an ex-boyfriend. When Miko least expects it, the old boyfriend shows up and ready to sweep her off her feet again. She wants to have her cake and eat it too. While Miko's doing her own thing, Julian is determined to become everything Miko ever wanted in a man and more, but will he go to extreme lengths to prove he's worthy of Miko's love? Julian Stevens soon finds out that he's capable of being more than he could ever imagine as he embarks on a journey that will change his life forever.

In Stores!!!

The police in New York and other major cities around the country are increasingly victimizing black men. The violence has escalated to deadly force, most of the time without justification. In this controversial book, noted author Richard Jeanty, tackles the problem of police brutality and the unfair treatment of Black men at the hands of police in New York City and the rest of the country.

In Stores!!!

Just when Darren thinks his relationship with Tina is flourishing, there is yet another hurdle on the road hindering their bliss. Tina saw a therapist for months to deal with her sexual addiction, but now Darren is wondering if she was ever treated completely. Darren has not been taking care of home and Tina's frustrated and agrees to a break-up with Darren. Will Darren lose Tina for good? Will Tina ever realize that Darren is the best man for her?

In Stores!!

Ronald Murphy was a player all his life until he and his best friend, Myles, met the women of their dreams during a brief vacation in South Beach, Florida. Sexual Jeopardy is story of trust, betrayal, forgiveness, friendship and hope.
In Stores!!!

Tina develops an insatiable sexual appetite very early in life. She
only loves her boyfriend, Darren, but he's too far away in college to satisfy her sexual needs.
Tina decides to get buck wild away in college
Will her sexual trysts jeopardize the lives of the men in her life?

In Stores!!!

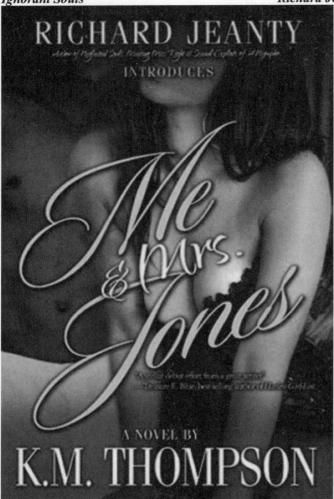

Faith Jones, a woman in her mid-thirties, has given up on ever finding love again until she met her son's best friend, Darius. Faith Jones is walking a thin line of betrayal against her son for the love of Darius. Will Faith allow her emotions to outweigh her common sense?

In Stores!!!

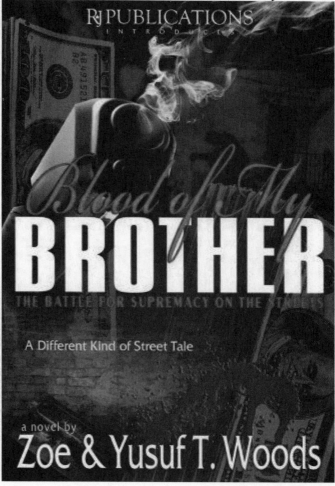

Roc was the man on the streets of Philadelphia, until his younger brother decided it was time to become his own man by wreaking havoc on Roc's crew without any regards for the blood relation they share. Drug, murder, mayhem and the pursuit of happiness can lead to deadly consequences. This story can only be told by a person who has lived it.

In Stores!!!

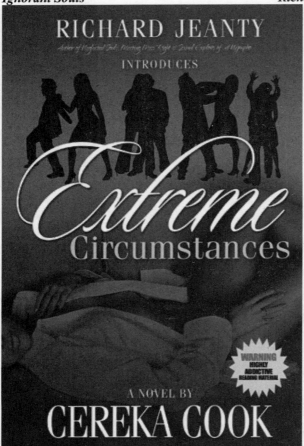

What happens when a devoted woman is betrayed? Come take a ride with Chanel as she takes her boyfriend, Donnell, to circumstances beyond belief after he betrays her trust with his endless infidelities. How long can Chanel's friend, Janai, use her looks to get what she wants from men before it catches up to her? Find out as Janai's gold-digging ways catch up with and she has to face the consequences of her extreme actions.

In Stores!!!

Violence, Intimidation and carnage are the order as Nathan and his brother set out to build the most powerful drug empires in Chicago. However, when God comes knocking, Nathan's conscience starts to surface. Will his haunted criminal past get the best of him?

In Stores!!

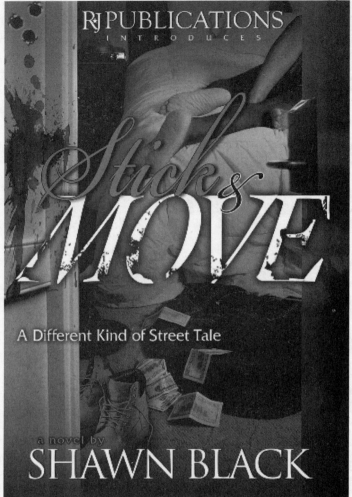

RJ PUBLICATIONS

INTRODUCES

Stick & MOVE

A Different Kind of Street Tale

a novel by

SHAWN BLACK

Yasmina witnessed the brutal murder of her parents at a young age at the hand of a drug dealer. This event stained her mind and upbringing as a result. Will Yamina's life come full circle with her past? Find out as Yasmina's crew, The Platinum Chicks, set out to make a name for themselves on the street.

In stores!!

Ashland's mother, Bianca, fights hard to suppress the truth from her daughter because she doesn't want her to marry Jordan, the grandson of an ex-lover she loathes. Ashland soon finds out how cruel and vengeful her mother can be, but what price will Bianca pay for redemption?

In stores!!

Malcolm is a wealthy virgin who decides to conceal his wealth From the world until he meets the right woman. His wealthy best friend, Dexter, hides his wealth from no one. Malcolm struggles to find love in an environment where vanity and materialism are rampant, while Dexter is getting more than enough of his share of women. Malcolm needs develop self-esteem and confidence to meet the right woman and Dexter's confidence is borderline arrogance.
Will bad boys like Dexter continue to take women for a ride?

Or will nice guys like Malcolm continue to finish last?

In Stores!!!

What happens when a woman's devotion to her fiancee is tested weeks before she gets married? What if her fiancee is just hiding behind the veil of ministry to deceive her? Find out as Sean Mitchell takes you on a journey you'll never forget into the lives of Angelica, Titus and Aurelius.

In Stores!!

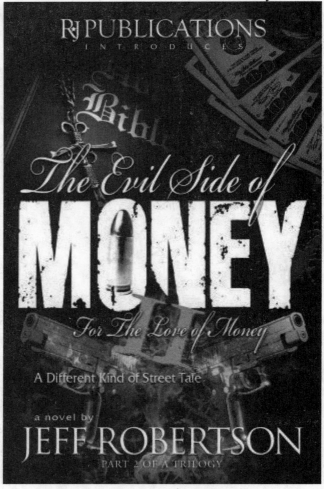

A beautigul woman from Bolivia threatens the existence of the drug empire that Nate and G have built. While Nate is head over heels for her, G can see right through her. As she brings on more conflict between the crew, G sets out to show Nate exactly who she is before she brings about their demise.

In Stores!!!

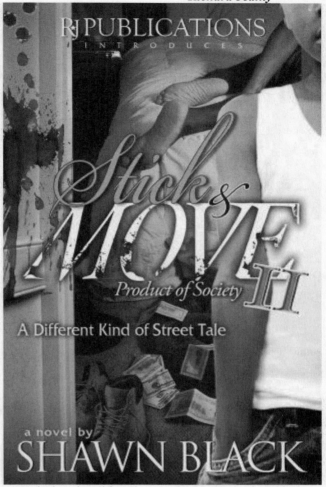

Scorcher and Yasmina's low key lifestyle was interrupted when they were taken down by the Feds, but their daughter, Serosa, was left to be raised by the foster care system. Will Serosa become a product of her environment or will she rise above it all? Her bloodline is undeniable, but will she be able to control it?

In Stores!!

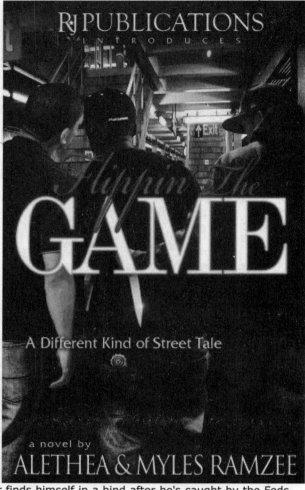

An ex-drug dealer finds himself in a bind after he's caught by the Feds. He has to decide which is more important, his family or his loyalty to the game. As he fights hard to make a decision, those who helped him to the top fear the worse from him. Will he get the chance to tell the govt. whole story, or will someone get to him before he becomes a snitch?

In Stores!!!

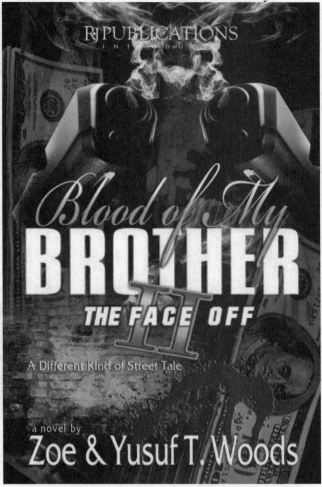

What will Roc do when he finds out the true identity of Solo? Will the blood shed come from his own brother Lil Mac? Will Roc and Solo take their beef to an explosive height on the street? Find out as Zoe and Yusuf bring the second installment to their hot street joint, Blood of My Brother.

In Stores!!!

Dave Richardson is enjoying success as his second book
became a New York Times best-seller. He left the life of
The Bedroom behind to settle with his family, but an
obsessed fan has not had enough of Dave and she will go to
great length to get a piece of him. How far will a woman go
to get a man that doesn't belong to her?

Coming September 2010

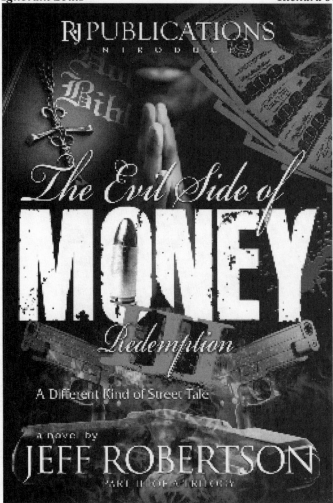

Forced to abandon the drug world for good, Nathan and G attempt to change their lives and move forward, but will their past come back to haunt them? This final installment will leave you speechless.

Coming November 2009

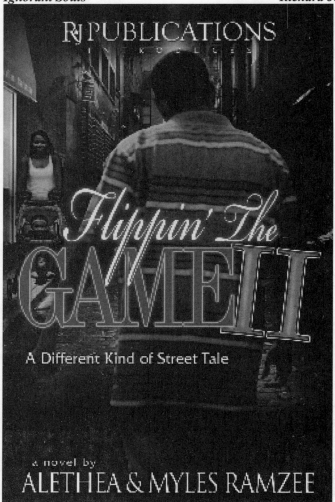

Nafys Muhammad managed to beat the charges in court, but will he beat them on the street? There will be many revelations in this story as betrayal, greed, sex scandal corruption and murder unravels throughout every page. Get ready for a rough ride.

Coming December 2009

Deon is at the mercy of a ruthless gang that kidnapped him. In a foreign land where he knows nothing about the culture, he has to use his survival instincts and his wit to outsmart his captors. Will the Hoodfellas show up in time to rescue Deon, or will Crazy D take over once again and fight an all out war by himself?

Coming March 2010

While Yasmina sits on death row awaiting her fate, her daughter, Serosa, is fighting the fight of her life on the outside. Her genetic structure that indirectly bins her to her parents could also be her downfall and force her to see that there's no way out!

Coming January 2010

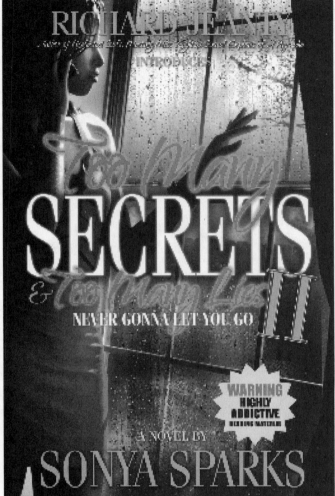

The drama continues as Deshun is hunted by Angela who still feels that ex-girlfriend Kayla is still trying to win his heart, though he brutally raped her. Angela will kill anyone who gets in her way, but is DeShun worth all the aggravation?

Coming September 2009

Buck Johnson was forced to make the best out of worst situation. He has witnessed the most cruel events in his life and it is those events who the man that he has become. Was the Johnson family ignorant souls through no fault of their own?

Coming October 2009

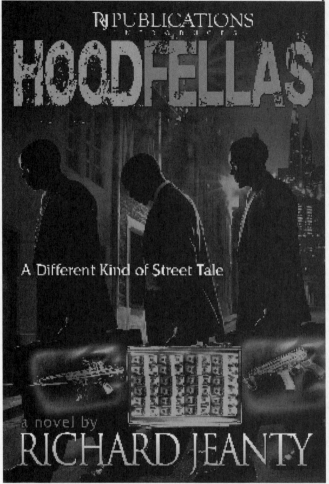

When an Ex-con finds himself destitute and in dire need of the basic necessities after he's released from prison, he turns to what he knows best, crime, but at what cost? Extortion, murder and mayhem drives him back to the top, but will he stay there?

In Stores !!!

What happens when someone falls insanely in love?
Stalking is just the beginning.
In Stores!!!

PUBLICATIONS
BRINGING EXCITEMENT, FUN AND JOY TO READING

Use this coupon to order by mail
1. Neglected Souls, Richard Jeanty $14.95
2. Neglected No More, Richard Jeanty $14.95
3. Ignorant Souls, Richard Jeanty $15.00, October 2009
4. Sexual Exploits of Nympho, Richard Jeanty $14.95
5. Meeting Ms. Right's Whip Appeal, Richard Jeanty $14.95
6. Me and Mrs. Jones, K.M Thompson $14.95
7. Chasin' Satisfaction, W.S Burkett $14.95
8. Extreme Circumstances, Cereka Cook $14.95
9. The Most Dangerous Gang In America, R. Jeanty $15.00
10. Sexual Exploits of a Nympho II, Richard Jeanty $15.00
11. Sexual Jeopardy, Richard Jeanty $14.95
12. Too Many Secrets, Too Many Lies, Sonya Sparks $15.00
13. Stick And Move, Shawn Black $15.00 Available
14. Evil Side Of Money, Jeff Robertson $15.00
15. Evil Side Of Money II, Jeff Robertson $15.00
16. Evil Side Of Money III, Jeff Robertson $15.00
17. Flippin' The Game, Alethea and M. Ramzee, $15.00 Available
18. Flippin' The Game II, Alethea and M. Ramzee, $15.00 Dec. 2009
19. Cater To Her, W.S Burkett $15.00
20. Blood of My Brother I, Zoe & Yusuf Woods $15.00
21. Blood of my Brother II, Zoe & Ysuf Woods $15.00
22. Hoodfellas, Richard Jeanty $15.00 available
23. Hoodfellas II, Richard Jeanty, $15.00 03/30/2010
24. The Bedroom Bandit, Richard Jeanty $15.00 Available
25. Mr. Erotica, Richard Jeanty, $15.00, Sept 2010
26. Stick N Move II, Shawn Black $15.00 Available
27. Stick N Move III, Shawn Black $15.00 Jan, 2010
28. Miami Noire, W.S. Burkett $15.00 Available
29. Insanely In Love, Cereka Cook $15.00 Available
30. Blood of My Brother III, Zoe & Yusuf Woods September 2009

Name_____
Address_____
City_____State_____Zip Code_____

Please send the novels that I have circled above.
Shipping and Handling: Free
Total Number of Books_____
Total Amount Due_____
          Buy 3 books and get 1 free. This offer is subject to change without notice.
Send institution check or money order (no cash or CODs) to:
RJ Publications
PO Box 300771
Jamaica, NY 11434
For more information please call 718-471-2926, or visit www.rjpublications.com

Please allow 2-3 weeks for delivery.

Use this coupon to order by mail
31. Neglected Souls, Richard Jeanty $14.95
32. Neglected No More, Richard Jeanty $14.95
33. Ignorant Souls, Richard Jeanty $15.00, October 2009
34. Sexual Exploits of Nympho, Richard Jeanty $14.95
35. Meeting Ms. Right's Whip Appeal, Richard Jeanty $14.95
36. Me and Mrs. Jones, K.M Thompson $14.95
37. Chasin' Satisfaction, W.S Burkett $14.95
38. Extreme Circumstances, Cereka Cook $14.95
39. The Most Dangerous Gang In America, R. Jeanty $15.00
40. Sexual Exploits of a Nympho II, Richard Jeanty $15.00
41. Sexual Jeopardy, Richard Jeanty $14.95
42. Too Many Secrets, Too Many Lies, Sonya Sparks $15.00
43. Stick And Move, Shawn Black $15.00 Available
44. Evil Side Of Money, Jeff Robertson $15.00
45. Evil Side Of Money II, Jeff Robertson $15.00
46. Evil Side Of Money III, Jeff Robertson $15.00
47. Flippin' The Game, Alethea and M. Ramzee, $15.00 Available
48. Flippin' The Game II, Alethea and M. Ramzee, $15.00 Dec. 2009
49. Cater To Her, W.S Burkett $15.00
50. Blood of My Brother I, Zoe & Yusuf Woods $15.00
51. Blood of my Brother II, Zoe & Ysuf Woods $15.00
52. Hoodfellas, Richard Jeanty $15.00 available
53. Hoodfellas II, Richard Jeanty, $15.00 03/30/2010
54. The Bedroom Bandit, Richard Jeanty $15.00 Available
55. Mr. Erotica, Richard Jeanty, $15.00, Sept 2010
56. Stick N Move II, Shawn Black $15.00 Available
57. Stick N Move III, Shawn Black $15.00 Jan, 2010
58. Miami Noire, W.S. Burkett $15.00 Available
59. Insanely In Love, Cereka Cook $15.00 Available
60. Blood of My Brother III, Zoe & Yusuf Woods September 2009

Name_____

Address_____

City_____State_____Zip Code_____

Please send the novels that I have circled above.
Shipping and Handling: Free
Total Number of Books_____
Total Amount Due_____
        Buy 3 books and get 1 free. This offer is subject to change without notice.
Send institution check or money order (no cash or CODs) to:
RJ Publications
PO Box 300771
Jamaica, NY 11434
For more information please call 718-471-2926, or visit www.rjpublications.com

Please allow 2-3 weeks for delivery.

PUBLICATIONS
BRINGING EXCITEMENT, FUN AND JOY TO READING

Use this coupon to order by mail
61. Neglected Souls, Richard Jeanty $14.95
62. Neglected No More, Richard Jeanty $14.95
63. Ignorant Souls, Richard Jeanty $15.00, October 2009
64. Sexual Exploits of Nympho, Richard Jeanty $14.95
65. Meeting Ms. Right's Whip Appeal, Richard Jeanty $14.95
66. Me and Mrs. Jones, K.M Thompson $14.95
67. Chasin' Satisfaction, W.S Burkett $14.95
68. Extreme Circumstances, Cereka Cook $14.95
69. The Most Dangerous Gang In America, R. Jeanty $15.00
70. Sexual Exploits of a Nympho II, Richard Jeanty $15.00
71. Sexual Jeopardy, Richard Jeanty $14.95
72. Too Many Secrets, Too Many Lies, Sonya Sparks $15.00
73. Stick And Move, Shawn Black $15.00 Available
74. Evil Side Of Money, Jeff Robertson $15.00
75. Evil Side Of Money II, Jeff Robertson $15.00
76. Evil Side Of Money III, Jeff Robertson $15.00
77. Flippin' The Game, Alethea and M. Ramzee, $15.00 Available
78. Flippin' The Game II, Alethea and M. Ramzee, $15.00 Dec. 2009
79. Cater To Her, W.S Burkett $15.00
80. Blood of My Brother I, Zoe & Yusuf Woods $15.00
81. Blood of my Brother II, Zoe & Ysuf Woods $15.00
82. Hoodfellas, Richard Jeanty $15.00 available
83. Hoodfellas II, Richard Jeanty, $15.00 03/30/2010
84. The Bedroom Bandit, Richard Jeanty $15.00 Available
85. Mr. Erotica, Richard Jeanty, $15.00, Sept 2010
86. Stick N Move II, Shawn Black $15.00 Available
87. Stick N Move III, Shawn Black $15.00 Jan, 2010
88. Miami Noire, W.S. Burkett $15.00 Available
89. Insanely In Love, Cereka Cook $15.00 Available
90. Blood of My Brother III, Zoe & Yusuf Woods September 2009

Name_____

Address_____

City_____State_____Zip Code_____

Please send the novels that I have circled above.
Shipping and Handling: Free
Total Number of Books_____
Total Amount Due_____
Buy 3 books and get 1 free. This offer is subject to change without notice.
Send institution check or money order (no cash or CODs) to:
RJ Publications
PO Box 300771
Jamaica, NY 11434
For more information please call 718-471-2926, or visit www.rjpublications.com

Please allow 2-3 weeks for delivery.

Use this coupon to order by mail
91. Neglected Souls, Richard Jeanty $14.95
92. Neglected No More, Richard Jeanty $14.95
93. Ignorant Souls, Richard Jeanty $15.00, October 2009
94. Sexual Exploits of Nympho, Richard Jeanty $14.95
95. Meeting Ms. Right's Whip Appeal, Richard Jeanty $14.95
96. Me and Mrs. Jones, K.M Thompson $14.95
97. Chasin' Satisfaction, W.S Burkett $14.95
98. Extreme Circumstances, Cereka Cook $14.95
99. The Most Dangerous Gang In America, R. Jeanty $15.00
100. Sexual Exploits of a Nympho II, Richard Jeanty $15.00
101. Sexual Jeopardy, Richard Jeanty $14.95
102. Too Many Secrets, Too Many Lies, Sonya Sparks $15.00
103. Stick And Move, Shawn Black $15.00 Available
104. Evil Side Of Money, Jeff Robertson $15.00
105. Evil Side Of Money II, Jeff Robertson $15.00
106. Evil Side Of Money III, Jeff Robertson $15.00
107. Flippin' The Game, Alethea and M. Ramzee, $15.00 Available
108. Flippin' The Game II, Alethea and M. Ramzee, $15.00 Dec. 2009
109. Cater To Her, W.S Burkett $15.00
110. Blood of My Brother I, Zoe & Yusuf Woods $15.00
111. Blood of my Brother II, Zoe & Ysuf Woods $15.00
112. Hoodfellas, Richard Jeanty $15.00 available
113. Hoodfellas II, Richard Jeanty, $15.00 03/30/2010
114. The Bedroom Bandit, Richard Jeanty $15.00 Available
115. Mr. Erotica, Richard Jeanty, $15.00, Sept 2010
116. Stick N Move II, Shawn Black $15.00 Available
117. Stick N Move III, Shawn Black $15.00 Jan, 2010
118. Miami Noire, W.S. Burkett $15.00 Available
119. Insanely In Love, Cereka Cook $15.00 Available
120. Blood of My Brother III, Zoe & Yusuf Woods September 2009

Name_____

Address_____

City_____State____Zip Code_____

Please send the novels that I have circled above.
Shipping and Handling: Free
Total Number of Books_____
Total Amount Due_____
Buy 3 books and get 1 free. This offer is subject to change without notice.
Send institution check or money order (no cash or CODs) to:
RJ Publications
PO Box 300771
Jamaica, NY 11434
For more information please call 718-471-2926, or visit www.rjpublications.com

Please allow 2-3 weeks for delivery.